DOWN FOR HER

A RICHES-TO-RAGS STEAMY ROMANCE

DESTINY DUNES SERIES

MELISSA CHAMBERS

Perry Evans Press

ISBN: 978-1732415652

Edited by Blue Otter Editing
Cover image from depositphotos

Also Available from Melissa Chambers:

Destiny Dunes Series:
Down for Her: A Riches-to-Rags Steamy Romance
Up for Seconds: A Second Chance Steamy Romance
Coming Around: A Friends-to-Lovers Steamy Romance
In His Heart: A Harbored Secrets Steamy Romance
Over the Moon: A Forced Proximity Steamy Romance
Under the Stars: An Enemies to Lovers Steamy Romance

Broussard Brothers Series:
Grumpy Beignet Boss: A Second Chance Steamy Romance
French Quarter Flirt: A Friends to Lovers Steamy Romance
Bourbon Street Bachelor: An Enemies to Lovers Steamy
Romance
Frenchmen Street First: A First Love Steamy Romance

Love Along Hwy 30A Series:
Seaside Sweets: A Steamy Small Town Beach Read
Seacrest Sunsets: A Steamy Opposites-Attract Beach Read
Seagrove Secrets-A Steamy Brother's Best Friend
Beach Read
WaterColor Wishes: A Steamy Enemies-to-Lovers Romance
Grayton Beach Dreams: A Steamy May-December Romance
Rosemary Beach Kisses: A Steamy Single Dad Romance
Christmas in Santa Rosa: A Steamy Second Chance
Romance

Young Adult titles:
The Summer Before Forever (Before Forever #1)
Falling for Forever (Before Forever #2)

Courting Carlyn (Standalone)
Two Boy Summer (Standalone)

1

KYLIE

As I open the car door to step into my new life, a wall of heat thrusts itself onto me. I could hold out a cup in this dense Florida humidity for a few minutes and have a full glass of liquid. But the weather is the least complicated obstacle I have to overcome.

As I shoulder the bag that has ridden shotgun beside me since I left Oklahoma yesterday, a guy among some twentysomethings on the porch of the identical housing unit beside the one I've been assigned gives a catcall. "Hey, gorgeous, screw them. Come see us. We've got beer."

I wonder what he means by *them*? I only have one roommate. Val is her name, according to the girl who checked me in at the Destiny Dunes housing office.

As I slip in the key card and step into my new home, the distinct smell of burnt rice assaults my nostrils and turns my grin into a grimace. At least three days' worth of dirty plates with caked-on goo litter the glass coffee table, and long tube socks drape across the faux-leather recliner. Dang, Val. I'm not the biggest clean freak on the planet, but even I have standards.

Those socks are humongous. A pair of super-sized sneakers topples over one another beside the recliner. Either she's got really big feet or her boyfriend is here. I hope he's not an asshole. That's my cynicism talking. But I have a right to be cynical about men right now.

Val must be home, because I hear the shower running. I start to walk into the kitchen, but something scurrying sends me stumbling backward. Even though I have a total of twenty-four dollars and sixty-four cents to my name, I'll most definitely be investing a portion of that into some sort of humane mousetrap.

I hear the shower turn off. "Dammit, Val," comes a guy's Southern drawl. "If you take my towel one more time, I'm gonna whip your ass."

I stiffen. If this is Val's boyfriend, I need to have a talk with her, because he's an ass.

"I don't suppose you've done any laundry either?" says the guy. Steps sound down the hallway, and then I hear what sounds like the opening of a dryer door. "Empty, of course." The dryer door closes, and then footsteps come my way. "You were here all damn day and you couldn't have—" The guy freezes in place as he catches sight of me.

Water drips down a six-pack of abs before my eyes. Words and phrases swirl around my brain, but my tongue doesn't seem to be working. I try desperately not to look farther south, but it's like being told not to scratch an itch.

He smooths his wet hair back, the muscles in his forearms and biceps colliding. "Can I help you?"

I look down, because boy, could he.

Bad Kylie. We will be having none of that. I am here to take my glorious job as pool girl and figure out my life. The last thing I need right now is another man. "You could start by putting on some clothes, please."

He gives me a lopsided grin that takes him from everyday hunk to full-on swoony heartbreaker. "No one's forcing you to look." He heads toward the kitchen, giving me a blessed view of two very scrumptious ass cheeks. "If you're looking for Val, he's in his bedroom."

His bedroom? Housing roomed me with a guy? I'm as progressive as the next person, but this seems a bit assuming. I hear the sound of kitchen drawers opening and closing. "Dammit. Are you serious?"

Stepping toward the kitchen, I peek in to find him rubbing a kitchen washcloth over his head and then across his shoulder and down his arm. I jog myself awake from my trance. "And who are you?"

"I'm Brett."

I look away, feeling busted for staring. "You're a friend of Val's?"

"Not at the moment. Ask me later, when I'm dry and this air-conditioning isn't blowing on my wet ass."

I rub my temple. "Okay, listen, I don't mean to be a bitch or anything, but we're going to have to lay down some ground rules."

He stops drying his chest and gives me the side-eye. "Ground rules?"

"I'm not sure why Housing has placed me with a man. I'm a forward thinker, so I will learn to get used to that if I must. But what I don't have to get used to is naked men walking around my home—at least ones who don't live here."

He narrows his gaze at me. "Who are you?"

I put my hands on my hips. "I am Val's new roommate." I lift my eyebrows in expectation of an apology.

He rests his naked ass against the counter, covering his

junk with the washrag. "Who told you that you were Val's new roommate?"

"Lauren in Housing," I say, as if everyone should know who Lauren in Housing is.

"All right. I don't know what the hell's going on, but let me get some clothes on and we'll go down to Housing and get this straightened out."

He moves past me and heads down the hallway. I follow him, trying to keep my gaze from his ass, but damn. "I'm sorry, what needs to be straightened out?"

He raps on a bedroom door. "Val," he says, and then opens it to find it empty. "Son of a bitch. He must have gone on down to the beach, which is why he took my damn towel." He goes into a bedroom and opens a dresser drawer, pulling out a pair of boxer briefs like he lives here or something. "They've assigned you to a housing unit that already has two people assigned to it."

I shift my weight from one leg to another, my mind searching everywhere for a nugget of knowledge that would help this make sense. "What?"

He opens his arms wide, the muscles in his biceps bulging. "This is my room. I'm Val's roommate."

I glance down the hallway at the number of doors, knowing the answer to my next question before I ask it. "Are there three bedrooms?"

"Nope," he says, pulling a pair of shorts up his legs.

I take a deep breath. "I'll just go back down to Housing and let them know they gave me the wrong key card or the wrong unit number or whatever."

"Did they give you unit number 1624?"

I nod.

"Did you use that key card to get into this unit?"

I nod again.

"Then it looks like somebody down there messed up."

"But Lauren told me that my roommate's name was Val."

He pulls a T-shirt over his head. "Therein lies the problem. When did you interview for your job here?"

"Last week." I cross my arms over my chest, lifting my chin. "Why?"

He sits on the bed, putting on his shoes. "Didn't you need to give a two-week notice at your current job?"

I shuffle my feet, looking down at them. "No, I didn't."

"What job did you take here?"

Frustration mounts in my chest. "Shouldn't we be getting down to Housing?"

He grabs a phone off the dresser and peers at it. "Shit."

"What?"

"It's after five. I hope they're not closed."

"Maybe someone's still there," I say, but in my heart, I know it's not true. Lauren was the only one in sight when I was there a few minutes ago, and she said she was going to be out of there as soon as she was done with me.

He picks up his keys. "Let's hope so. If not, you might need to find somewhere else to stay tonight."

"I don't have anywhere else to stay tonight," I say, the volume in my tone rising.

"What about a friend or something?"

I rub my temple, my chest tightening. "You're the only person I know here."

He lowers his chin, his hazel eyes bearing into mine. "You don't know me."

"Exactly."

"Come on. Let's just go and see if anyone's there."

I follow him down the hallway, my heart on pins and needles, because unless I can find a hotel room for about ten dollars, I'm completely sunk.

2

BRETT

Sometimes I feel like I'm cursed. All I wanted to do was get showered, have a towel sitting there when I got out, and then open the one damn beer I allow myself on weekend nights. And now I'm in my vehicle driving over to Housing, knowing there's not gonna be anyone there.

The brunette huddles close to the door panel of my truck, cutting her eyes at me like I'm gonna bite her. Not that I wouldn't mind biting her. She's nice-looking. Despite her bossy attitude, there's something interesting about her face, the way her lips sort of form a little heart, and her eyes are kind of downturned on the sides. It makes her look soft, like she's not capable of harming a fly. I wouldn't kick her out of bed.

She catches me looking and glances around the inside of my truck. "What kind of car is this?"

"International Scout."

"It's...old."

"'Seventy-five model."

"Does it break down a lot?"

"Nothing I can't fix."

I stare at the road as we ride in silence, but I can feel her eyes on me. I meet her gaze and she glances away quickly. I've never seen so much leg fill up my front seat.

I pull into the empty lot. "This is not looking good."

She is out of the car and hustling up to the entryway before I can get the engine cut off. She tugs on the door but it doesn't open.

I meet up with her, and she turns to me, panic in her eyes. "Is there an after-hours number I can call or something?"

I glance around. "There's maintenance, but they don't really do much unless your toilet's overflowing."

Her expression crumbles as the color drains from her face.

I shut my eyes because I can't take that wounded-bird expression. "Look, it's not a big deal. Just get a cheap hotel. There's a dozen around here." She bites on her lip and nods, her eyes starting to water. Shit. I let out a deep breath. "Is there something I can help you with? Name of a hotel?"

She shakes her head. "No, it's fine. I'll figure something out."

"Did your wallet get stolen or something?"

"No, I have it, there's just not anything in it. Listen, I'm sorry that I crashed into your Friday night. Just take me back to your place, and I'll get my car."

As I follow her to my car, I stare at the back of her head like it's gonna give me answers. Why would she not have a credit card in her wallet? She looks like the kind of woman who takes really good care of herself. She dresses like the moms who I talk to at work about their kids' occupational therapy plans and strategies—athletic clothes, but expensive-looking ones like they get from one of those stores that has fruit in its name.

Whatever is going on with her is none of my business. But I'm not the kind of guy who can just walk away from a lady in need. My mom would knock me upside the head.

I regret my next words before they come out of my mouth. "Do you need a place to stay?"

She meets my gaze, those worried blue eyes cutting through my heart. She looks away. "No, I'm fine. Just...let's go back to your place."

I put her in the truck, and we ride in silence. Her eyebrows have formed a permanent band of worry. She stares straight through the asphalt, her mind looking to be working a hundred miles an hour. She's so worried about her next steps that she's forgotten to be wary of me.

She gets out of my truck and walks to her car, fumbling with her keys. She's such a ball of nerves that she drops them on the ground, and her hand shakes as she reaches down to pick them up.

I beg my feet to go toward the front door, leaving her to deal with her own shit, but they simply won't go. Cursed. "Look, you can sleep in my bed tonight."

She frowns at me.

I roll my eyes. "And I'll sleep on the couch."

"What about Val?"

"What the hell will he care? You'll be in my room."

She scratches her eyebrow. "Is he...cool?"

I cock my head to the side. "Do you mean is he going to sneak into your bed in the middle of the night?"

It's her turn to roll her eyes, then she concedes. "Well, is he?"

"No. He's not like that."

She puts her hands on her hips. "What is he like?"

"Gay."

"Oh," she says, considering this new info like it's a game changer, and then she closes her eyes and shakes her head quickly. "This is just ridiculous. I'll figure something else out."

"What, you don't trust me?" I say, giving her the grin that usually makes pissed-off women forget they're mad.

She purses her lips, looking me up and down. "No."

I toss up my hands, backing away. "No skin off my back. Good luck finding somewhere to stay." I turn around and walk inside, trying to play it cool, but just as I'm about to close the door behind me, my cold, withered-up heart experiences a temporary shock of warmth.

She lifts her chin, swiping at her eyes as she marches around to her driver's-side door. She gets inside and sits, hands on the wheel, looking lost and desperate.

"Shit," I say aloud, my need to help the women in my life nudging me back out the door. I can just see the look on Tori's face when she finds out I've taken in a stray for the weekend.

I walk around to her window, peering in to find her with her head against the steering wheel, eyes closed. I rap gently on the window.

She sits up, eyes wide, and then powers the window down. "I'm sorry. I'm going."

"Come on in. I'm not a serial killer and neither is Val."

She narrows her gaze at me, seeming to try her best to justify walking into this house with me.

Tiff from up the street walks down the sidewalk of my front lawn, grinning at me. "Hey, Brett."

Kylie looks away from me, her expression worried and defeated.

"Tiff, come here," I say.

Her grin widens as she comes my way. "What's up? You going to the bonfire later?"

I grin back. "We'll see about that. Do you have a free couch tonight? This is Kylie. She needs a place to stay for the weekend."

Kylie waves her hands. "No, no. I'm fine. I'm just gonna—"

"I wish I did," Tiff says. "My girlfriends are coming in for the weekend. We're gonna be on top of each other." She waggles her eyebrows at me. "You should come over."

I look her up and down. "I damn well may take you up on that."

Tiff winks and starts to walk away.

"Hey," I say. "I'm trying to convince Kylie that it's safe to stay here with Val and me. Tell her I'm not gonna stab her to death in her sleep if she stays here."

Tiff walks over and peers into the car at Kylie. "Are you afraid of him?"

"No, of course not," Kylie says, shifting in her seat.

Tiff rests her arm on the doorframe. "I know about two dozen girls who would give their eyeteeth to stay in this house for the weekend. I'm about to ditch my girlfriends and trade places with you."

I pull her away from the car. "All right. You can stand down now."

She puts her hand on my waist then slowly moves it across my abs. "If you need someone to tell you a bedtime story, you know where to find me."

"I sure do. See you on the beach later."

"You can meet my friends."

"Looking forward to it."

She wiggles her fingers at me and heads down the sidewalk, putting a shake in that walk for me to enjoy. Kylie clears her throat, getting my attention.

I put my hand on the doorframe. "Do you trust me now?"

She closes her eyes, gripping the steering wheel, and then lets out a hard breath. "Not really." She opens her door.

We stand face-to-face. She's tall. I'm just an inch or two taller.

"Thank you," she says.

"No problem." We head inside, and I walk to my bedroom and set her bags on the floor. She stops in the doorway, shifting her body weight from one side to the other. "What?" I ask.

"Nothing. It's just, I'm pretty sure this is my father's actual worst nightmare."

I huff a laugh. "What, he thinks you've never spent the night in a strange guy's room?"

Her face turns red, and she slides inside, lifting her bag onto the bed.

"Ah," I say and start to walk out.

She jerks her head around. "Ah, what?"

"You haven't ever spent the night in a strange guy's room, have you?"

"What does that matter?"

"It doesn't matter. It just helps me understand you better."

"Oh, so you think since I haven't had a one-night stand that you know me?"

"I know something about you."

"You don't know anything about me."

"Then tell me something about you I should know."

She stares at me like she's trying to gauge whether or not

she can trust me. She should definitely decide negative on that. "You go first," she says.

"There's nothing you need to know about me other than I'm not going to slip into this bed with you in the middle of the night...unless you ask me to."

She huffs a humorless laugh. "No worries about that."

"Yeah, I didn't think so. Shower's through there, but good luck finding a towel." I shut the door and head out for a beer.

3

KYLIE

I collapse onto Brett's bed and drop my face into my hands. Closing my eyes, I inhale a deep breath. What am I doing here? I've only second-guessed myself eight thousand times, but I've come too far to turn back now. I've made a statement by walking away. I won't beg my father for help, and I won't be like my mother and sacrifice my soul...at least not from now on.

Even so, this could be my early demise. Tomorrow's headline could read, "Woman Found Hacked Up in Guy's Bathroom."

If Brett is a psychopath, he's a damn good-looking one—not that I'm noticing or anything. The very last thing I need is to get mixed up with another man. But he's kind of hard to look away from with his whole young Tom Hardy thing going on. And he must be decent at heart, because he is helping me, albeit reluctantly.

I check my phone for messages and find one from Joshua. I close my eyes and let out the exhale to end all exhales. This is definitely not what I want to deal with at this moment.

Your dad called me today. He wants me to talk some sense into you.

I can't help but get a little satisfaction out of this. My dad's desperate. He can feel his control slipping away. Joshua texts again.

Is it true he cut off your credit cards and bank account? That's hard-core.

My lip curls up in disgust as I refrain from responding. He doesn't deserve my words.

Samantha says you're not staying with her anymore. Where'd you go?

I just sit there staring at the phone, the rage building up in my gut once again.

Come on, just tell me so I don't have to bug all our friends with our dirty laundry.

I stand up and throw the phone on the bed. "Your dirty laundry, Joshua. Yours."

I head into the bathroom. It's boy-gross, but not filthy like the rest of the house, which is a supreme relief. I shower the road trip off my body and out of my hair and then put on a lounge set. I pull out a pack of peanut butter crackers I got from the convenience store where I filled up my car with three dollars' worth of gas. I didn't even know you could do such a thing till I tried it and it worked. In my previous life, I just let the pump go until it cut off.

I've been lying here at least an hour, obsessively going through my former friends' Instagram pages when I hear a knock at the front door. I sit still, hoping they will go away, but then the door opens. Whoever it is comes into the house.

"Brett!" I hear a female voice shout. Footsteps sound down the hallway, and I brace as the door flings open. "Naptime's over. Get your—" A short girl sporting a messy bun—

dark on top, auburn on bottom—stares at me. "Shit. Sorry." She frowns and then holds up her hand. "Relax. I'm not one of the many. Is he in the bathroom?"

"Um, no."

She checks her phone. "Asshole's ignoring his phone. We're supposed to go to the bonfire together, but screw it, I guess."

As she goes to shut the door again, I say, "I'm not either."

She stops and eyes me.

"I'm not one of the many. I'm Kylie."

She just looks at me funny.

"He's helping me out. I needed a place to stay."

This seems to register with her. "Of course he is. Where did you come from?"

I sit up in the bed. "Oklahoma. I thought this was my housing unit. I mean, Lauren in Housing gave me the key card and unit number for this place, but clearly I'm not supposed to be here. I start work at the resort on Monday."

"Thanks for the info, but your business is your own. You don't know where he is?"

"No, he left out of here maybe an hour, hour and a half ago."

"What about Val?"

"I haven't met him yet."

"All right. Well, if Brett gets back, tell him I went on to the bonfire without him. I'm Tori."

"Will definitely do."

She goes to shut the door and then scrunches up her face like she's dreading her next words. "Do you want to come to the bonfire with me?"

"Oh, no, thank you. I'm good right here."

She lets out a sigh and puts her hand on her hip. "Get

up. Come on. You can't spend your first weekend here holed up in this nasty-ass place."

"No, really, I'm fine."

"You don't go to parties?"

"I do, of course," I say, sounding very unconvincing. Something tells me if I mention to this girl that the parties I go to are typically catered and at someone's McMansion, I'll get an eye roll.

She shakes her head. "Man, have you happened into the wrong house. Come on. I'm offering to help you. I don't do that a lot."

As much as I want to stay in this bed, I know that part of all of this distance from my father and Joshua and finding my own place in life means I have to venture into the wild, and this girl seems like she would be a good guide.

"Okay, just give me a minute to change," I say.

"I'll be waiting on the front porch."

Most of my clothes are in my other suitcases in the trunk of my car. I don't want to be assuming by breaking all those out. So I dig in my smaller bag for anything, and I come up with a knee-length flowy skirt and heather-gray V-neck. I'll call it hippy chic and see if I can pull it off. I head out to meet her, and she looks me up and down as she hands me a can of beer. "You're kind of dressy. Are you sure you don't want to put on some shorts? It's the beach."

The only shorts I have are the ones Lauren gave me at check-in that sport the resort logo, so I say, "I'm comfortable in this skirt." She shrugs and we head down the steps.

"Do you work here?" I ask.

"Yeah. I'm a recreational therapist."

"Oh. What does a recreational therapist do?"

"I put together treatment plans for the kids. Brett and I consult with one another, usually one or both of us with their therapists at home so we can provide the best care for them possible here for the week or two, however long they're staying."

I nod as if this all sounds normal. But I've got to admit, I'm confused. "And you do that here?" I say, pointing at the ground.

She looks at me funny. "Yeah. Are you familiar with what this resort is set up for?"

I clear my throat. "Maybe not."

"Families who have kids with disabilities or who need accommodations come here for vacation. The resort is set up with them in mind."

"Oh. Wow," I say, feeling ridiculous for having missed this in my two minutes of research I did for the job I applied for. I simply searched *Jobs in Florida Panhandle with employee housing* and thought the stars had aligned when these people responded. "Shouldn't all resorts have them in mind?"

"I imagine most all resorts are ADA compliant, but we go past the minimum requirements. Kids Company is a place where parents can drop their kids and feel completely comfortable that they're in the hands of trained professionals who have made an effort to get to know them before they even arrive."

"That's amazing. Truly. And Brett...is he also a recreational therapist?"

"He's an occupational therapist." She eyes me. "What job did you take here?"

My neck heats up. "Pool attendant?" I say, like I'm asking permission.

She shrugs as if accepting my fate and takes a sip of her beer as we walk down the sidewalk.

"Tori!" shouts a guy from a porch at one of the housing

units that looks exactly like Brett's. "Skip the bonfire. Bring your friend here and hang with us." Tori simply holds up her middle finger and we keep walking.

She leads us to the end of the street, where we cut through the backyards of some condominiums and make our way to the top of a flight of stairs. Down below, a bonfire swells with flames licking up toward the sky. People our age swarm around laughing, dancing, and hooking up. I haven't been to a party like this since college. The get-togethers in our friend group back home involve expensive bottles of wine, hors d'oeuvres, and couples sitting around debating Turks and Caicos versus Tuscany.

Tori grins at me. "Come on, pool girl. Let's find some boys who can hold our interest."

We scurry down the beach access stairs, and when we reach the bottom, Tori kicks off her flip-flops near a pile of shoes, so I follow suit. My toes melt into sand as fine as powdered sugar. "Wow, I've never felt sand like this before," I say.

Tori grins. "Welcome to the panhandle."

I follow her into the party, where a cute guy grabs her and pulls her to him like he's going to kiss her. She pushes him away and then pulls him down to her by his T-shirt, kissing him on her terms. She turns to me, smiling. "This is Logan. He bartends at Big Fish Pub at the Circle. So if you ever need a free drink, he's your guy."

I nod, my neck going warm, because he's super cute. Do they breed them cuter in Florida? "The Circle...that's where they have all the restaurants and games and stuff?"

"Yep," he says, wrapping his arm around Tori's waist.

"Kylie's new," Tori says. "She starts Monday."

"What are you doing?" he asks.

"I'm starting at the lagoon pool," I say, avoiding the inevitable.

"Lifeguard?" he asks.

The pit of my stomach sinks. "No, pool attendant."

He shrugs. "That's cool. Your drinks are definitely free."

"Like she wants to hang with the tourists." Tori covers the side of her mouth and points at him, whispering, "Weak."

Logan picks her up and tosses her over his shoulder. "I'll show you weak." He runs off with her as she squeals at him, pounding on his back.

I take a deep breath, realizing I'm totally solo. I knew I should never have left Brett's room. I look around at all the people, feeling like a whale in a river.

My eye is drawn to a couple. The girl is leaned up against a WaveRunner and the guy has his legs spread apart, leaning in toward her. She grins up at him like she'd rather be nowhere else on the planet. He runs his hand across her cheek, resting it on the back of her neck, smoothing his thumb over her jawline. My stomach fizzes like I can understand what she's experiencing.

I've never once had a guy make me feel that dominated. My relationship with Joshua has been so settled from the beginning, so ordinary...predictable.

My heartbeat pounds for her as he takes her hand, so confident, knowing she's totally ready to surrender herself to him. They start to walk away when he turns his head toward the fire, and heat rushes through my whole body as I realize it's Brett. His hair's lighter now that it's dry.

He catches my gaze and smiles at me like the dog that got the bone.

"Hey." I turn to find a guy who has come up to me, tall, dark-haired, and so gorgeous I think I might need to step backward to take him in. His hair is cut short like a business guy, but with just enough wavy length to keep him youthful. His body's tall and broad like a tight end.

He doesn't fit in with this crowd. He's way cleaner cut than the rest of them. He reminds me of home.

"Hi," I say.

"I don't recognize you. Are you here with a friend who works at Destiny Dunes?"

"I just got a job there. I start on Monday. Do you work there?"

"Yeah. I'm Jack." He proffers his hand, and I take it and shake it.

"Kylie," I say. "What do you do at the resort?"

"I work in Business Affairs. Been here ever since I left college."

"When was that?" I ask, a sneaky way to gauge his age.

He closes one eye, thinking. "Five years now, I guess?"

"Where did you go to school?"

"Cornell."

Definitely feeling more at home with him, but I've got to remind myself that my old life is behind me now. I'm a pool attendant, and that's how this guy will see me. "What brought you all the way down here?"

"I'm from Atlanta. This is close enough to home where I can head up there for a weekend if I want but far enough away not to make me crazy." He tilts his cup toward me. "Where are you from?"

"Edmond, Oklahoma."

He stares at me blankly, nodding.

"I went to OU in Norman though."

"Ah," he says, on more familiar ground. Most guys know OU because of their stellar football team. "You're far from home, aren't you?"

I run my toe through the sand. "You have no idea. So why Cornell?"

"It's actually the number one school in the country for Hospitality Management."

"So you knew going in that's what you wanted to do?"

"It's the family business. My dad's pissed 'cause I didn't come to work in his hotel in Atlanta."

I chuckle. "I guess we have pissed dads in common. Mine is mad that I actually moved across the country from him."

He holds up his cup to mine. "To pissed dads."

I smile and touch my cup to his. "May they mind their own business."

He smiles at me like I've just crossed a line from stranger to friend. "Do you live at the resort?"

What a loaded question. "Yes, I hope so, at least. They screwed up my housing reservation, and I walked in on a naked guy today."

"Whoa," he says with a concerned look. "Bet that was more than you bargained for. You okay?"

His reaction of concern instead of laughter is comforting to me in a strange way. I feel like I've been playing defense since I stepped into Brett's house. It's a nice break. "Yeah, I'm fine. Thanks for asking, though."

"Who'd you walk in on?"

"This guy named Brett. His roommate's name is Val, but I haven't met him yet."

Jack sports a rueful smile and hangs his head, shaking it.

"You know them?" I ask.

"I know Hargrove...Brett, I mean. Yeah." He pockets his hand, lowering his chin. The expression on his face has soured.

"Not a fan?" I ask, because clearly, this guy has some beef with him.

"It's a long story. Did you get the housing mistake figured out?"

"No, actually. We went down to the housing office, but it was already locked up tight. Brett's letting me stay in his room until Monday morning, when we can get it all cleared up."

He huffs a laugh. "I bet he is."

"Nothing's happening between him and me. Trust me."

"It's him I wouldn't trust," Jack says, looking past me. "Speak of the devil."

I swivel my neck as a hand sweeps across my back and rests on my hip. Brett stands beside me, and my traitorous girl parts tingle from his touch. I'm this close to pulling away, but I'm too curious to see what his game is.

Jack returns Brett's glare. "Hargrove."

"Massey. I see you met Kylie. She's staying with me this weekend."

"Thanks to Housing's screwup." Jack turns to me with a wink. "I'll call them tomorrow and get it straightened out for you."

I'm about to open my mouth when Brett says, "No, thanks. I'll handle it Monday morning."

"Or I could call Robert right now and she could be snoozing in her own bed tonight," Jack says.

"It's handled," Brett says. "Mind your own damn business. Why are you even here? I thought guys in your position didn't make it down to the trenches."

"Robert likes me to mingle with our employees. Keep my eye on morale, report back to him. You know, general right-hand-man duties."

Brett lets a huff of air out of his nostrils, kind of like a dragon.

Tori slides into our tumultuous circle and takes my hand. "I think our newbie's had enough of this testosterone for the moment. Come with me, girl. I'll get you a drink."

She pulls me from the man sandwich toward a keg with a bag of plastic cups beside it. "I take it they're not besties?" I ask Tori.

"That's an understatement. It's kind of my fault though. I had a thing with Jack last year that ended badly. Brett's like the overprotective brother I never asked for." She grabs a couple of cups from the bag.

"Like a brother?" I ask, my curiosity getting the better of me.

She gives me a knowing grin as she pumps the keg. "Brett and I have known each other since we were little. We grew up in the same trailer park."

I nod as if I've known lots of trailer parks in my time.

She rolls her eyes like she sees through me. "We're both seven years older than our brothers. The two of us raised the two of them for the most part. So I guess he's more like a husband than a brother." She scrunches up her face. "Without the benefits, of course."

I cut my eyes at her. "Never?"

"Fuck no. I was never interested, and besides that screwing our relationship up with sex was the last thing either of us needed back then. And now, it's just way too late for anything like that. Besides, I could never be with a guy like him."

"Like what?"

She nods, focused on something. I turn to find Brett talking to a different girl from the one he kissed just a little while ago. He takes her hand and pulls her to his chest, which she falls right into like she's stepped into quicksand.

"He definitely likes the ladies," I say.

"Ya think? Come on. I'll introduce you around."

Tori diligently introduces me to more people than I can keep up with, telling me what part of the resort they work in. I do a better job remembering departments than names, but I appreciate her efforts.

I wish this wasn't the case, but I can't keep my eyes off of Brett. He stands near the fire, invested in yet another *honey* when I notice him look at his phone and step away from her. I start to roll my eyes, thinking he's choosing a booty call over the girl in front of him, but the serious turn of his expression throws me. He puts the phone to his ear, running his hand through his hair, frowning. I can't put my finger on why I'm so interested in him, other than his overall hotness. But with every minute of this night, I'm finding myself more and more intrigued.

4

BRETT

"Don't panic. Nothing's wrong, honey," my mom says by way of greeting. "I just wanted to see if you would pick up Mimi's prescription on your way over tomorrow."

"I know. I got your text. Does she need it now?"

"It can wait until tomorrow. It's Friday night. I'm sure you're out with your friends."

"Where's Matthew?"

"He left out of here as soon as I got home from work."

I walk even farther away from the party, trying not to get irritated with my brother. He's got his life just like I've got mine. I get it. But I've been living in that trailer since we moved there from the military base when I was seven years old. He's old enough now to take on some of the responsibilities I've borne since our dad died twenty years ago.

"Mom, we agreed that you would call on me in emergency situations."

"I know, and this is not an emergency."

"Yeah, but if Mimi needs her medication, I consider that an emergency."

She lets out a sigh. "I tried to pick it up on my way home from work, but it wasn't ready yet. I used to run out and leave her if it was just gonna be a minute, but I've quit doing that."

"Next time let's not play this game. Just text me and tell me to go pick up the prescription."

"I swear, honey, if I ever get like this and you don't put me in a nursing home, I'll kill you."

"You're one to talk."

This is an ongoing argument between my mother and me. Anytime I try to talk my mom into the nursing home, I talk myself out of it just as quickly. Neither one of us can bring ourselves to turn Mimi over to a home, so between the two of us, we're paying for a sitter to be with her all day while my mom works. Between that and Matthew's tuition, it's tough for me to keep up.

"I'll be there in an hour," I say.

"Take your time. She's not going anywhere."

We end the call, and the brunette who's sleeping in my bed tonight walks my way, frowning at me in concern. I can't deal with her wounded sincerity right now. "I was just heading out...unless you have something else in mind." I nod toward the bed of a rusted-out sailboat, like this uptight, classy-looking woman would ever dream of getting nasty with me a few feet away from forty or fifty of our colleagues.

She peers inside the sailboat. "I think I'll pass."

I huff a laugh at her and start to walk away, but she grabs my arm. The move surprises me so much I turn to meet her gaze.

"I know you're way too cool to have actual feelings and stuff, but if you want to talk about anything, I'll listen," she says.

I'm so taken aback by her offer that I'm tempted to start talking. I could tell her about how my every thought is consumed with taking care of my mom, my brother, and my grandma. I could tell her how every time I talk to my mom, I'm checking for hints of her possibly drinking or using again, and how I haven't had a decent night's sleep since my dad died when I was seven. I could tell her about how I can't fathom a day when I'll be able to relax, knowing everyone's safe, because our lives are a carefully stacked house of cards that could collapse at any moment without warning. But instead, I say, "What makes you think I've got some big problem you can solve?"

"You just looked stressed or something."

"I'm not." I back away. "I'm fine."

"Sure thing." She glances around. "I think I'm gonna head to your room. I'm tired. It's been a long day on the road. Is that where you're going?"

I think about the three girls I've been bouncing between tonight and watch a night of stress release float away. It's not like my heart was into it with any of them. And I already lost the first one to Kylie as it was. I was all set to head back to her condo when I caught sight of Kylie talking to Jack Massey. I couldn't let that go uninterrupted. "Yeah, I'll walk you back." We head toward our pile of shoes.

"I'm not taking you away from your many conquests, am I? Were you going for a foursome?"

This makes me grin. "You were watching me tonight?"

"No, of course not. It's just a small party. You kept getting in my line of sight." As we search for our shoes, she says, "Tori told me you and she grew up together, but she didn't say where."

"Wabash...just North of here."

"What's in Wabash?" she asks as we head up the steps.

"Not much of anything."

We reach the top of the stairs and walk in silence a minute, and then she says, "So I hear you're an occupational therapist. How'd you get into that?"

So she's one of those. No comfortable silences. "It's sort of a long story."

"Longer than the walk from here to your housing unit?"

I think about whether or not I want to get into this with her. The last time I shared private info about my family with a girl, it didn't end well.

"I'm sorry," she says. "Was that an intrusive question?"

I shake my head as we step onto the sidewalk, realizing I'm being paranoid. She's just making conversation. She's not Madison. "I found this place when I was sixteen, actually."

"You've been working here since you were sixteen?"

"Yeah. I started out at the Circle busing tables for one of the restaurants, then I moved to games."

"That must've been a little more fun," she says with a smile that threatens to make me return one. "How did you make the move to occupational therapy from games? That seems like quite the leap."

I'm damn sure not gonna tell her about my brother. I don't even know her. "Just did."

She looks at me strangely.

"What?" I ask.

"I don't know. It's just your personality seems to be at odds with itself."

"Excuse me?"

"On one hand, you're this guy who wants to devote his life to helping little kids, and on the other hand, you have three girls on the hook in the course of about an hour and a half."

"I don't know what to tell you," I say, picking up my pace.

She catches up with me. "Tell me you'll slow down. I think I'm about to blow out a strap on my sandal."

I stop and turn to her, and she just smiles at me like she got me.

I roll my eyes and start walking again. "You ask a lot of questions."

"That's typically what people do to get to know one another."

"Why would we need to do that?" I ask.

She's silent for a second, and then I give her a partial smile to indicate I'm kidding. It's her turn to roll her eyes.

I pull my keys out of my pocket as we approach my car, nodding toward the front door of our unit. "You've got your own key card, at least for now."

She pulls it out of her pocket. "I assume you're off to satisfy girl number four?"

"Something like that," I say. "See you in the morning."

Just as I'm about to slide into my front seat, I hear the voice of my sworn enemy. "You're headed home early, too?" But Jack's not talking to me. He's walking on the lawn toward Kylie, who's at the front door now.

She walks in his direction, saying something in return, but I can't make it out. What's that asshole doing up here, anyway? He lives in a high-rise on the beach. He's clearly not funding his brother's college and his grandma's health-care. He was probably walking Bailey or Simone home since he came from the direction of their unit.

They stand on my front lawn, smiling at each other like idiots. Are they flirting? Fuck, why do I care?

I start my vehicle and back out of the driveway, leaving the resort and heading toward the pharmacy. I just need to focus on my grandma and getting her meds...and I need to quit wondering if Kylie's gonna invite that asshole into my house.

5

KYLIE

I've been awake for half an hour, but I'm almost afraid to move from the bed. Val and Brett must both be sound asleep, because you can pretty much hear a pin drop in here...or a mouse scurrying. Maybe one or both of them never made it home last night.

I stare at the ceiling, unable to believe I'm in a strange guy's bed, who's probably in some strange girl's bed. If Joshua could see me now, he'd... I wonder what he'd even do? Would he care?

I check my phone. No more messages from Joshua, but there is one from Samantha.

Are you doing okay? Just checking in.

I'm tempted to tell her where I am and what's happening, because it's all so bizarre, but I don't need her trying to send me money. She already gave me two hundred dollars. She tucked it in my purse as we were saying goodbye the other day. "Just in case," she had said. Little did she know that money has been my saving grace.

I text back. *I'm good. Settled in.*

I text her a little about the resort and the accommodations they provide to kids with disabilities.

Wow. Sounds like you landed in the right spot. All that experience at your dad's company will soon be put to very good use! I'm so excited for this venture in your life! Off to greener pastures!

Ugh. I'm regretting my white lies to my closest friend—the only loyal friend I have left. I just didn't want her to worry. If she knew I was taking a job as pool attendant, she would never have let me leave without a fight. She might have even done something like contacted my dad for help. I need to do this on my own. I need for her to believe everything's okay.

I text her back a smiley face and then stick my phone in my purse. I wander down the hallway, walking softly until I pass Val's room and find it empty. I head to the living room, peeking over the back of the couch, and it's unoccupied as well. I've been hiding in Brett's room and the whole place has been deserted, probably all night.

Venturing into the kitchen, I open the refrigerator door and close it right away when I see it's nothing but a biohazard in there. I'm not sure I can survive this place, even for a weekend.

I open the cabinet under the sink to see if there are any cleaning products, and I find a caddy with rubber gloves, floor cleaner, spray cleaner, toilet bowl cleaner and brush, sponges, dishwasher detergent, and a dish scrubber. There's a bow around it and a note attached that says, *Val, clean your floors at least once a week,* por favor, mijo. *Love, Mamá.*

I can't help a chuckle, thinking of my own mother leaving a note like this. I'm pretty sure she assumes someone magically handles that for everyone. She's always had someone clean her house...and so have I, for that matter.

It hits me that I could clean. Why can't I? Sure, I've never done it before, but it can't be that hard. The supplies are sitting right here.

I pull out the caddy and set it on the counter, investigating the bottles. Then I look around at the carnage of this place. You can't actually clean surfaces until those surfaces are empty. I put on the rubber gloves and grab the trash can. I dump in day/week/month-old food from both the living room and the kitchen. Then I load the dishwasher full of nasty, caked-on pans and put soap in.

I find a brand-new broom in the closet with the cardboard still on it and sweep the floors in the kitchen and throughout the small dining room, living room, and hallway. I squirt toilet bowl cleaner all over the commode and then stare perplexedly into the water with the black mold on the sides. "How does that get clean?" I ask myself.

I take to Google, and thanks to a very helpful video, I find that the cleaner actually goes into the water. I decide to let that soak a minute while I figure out how to get the rest of the cleaner off the outside of the toilet. I'm pretty sure there's no video for that.

I hear the front door open, and then two guys' voices sound through the house. I sincerely hope neither of them has to pee right away. I walk into the hallway holding up my gloved hands. "I'm cleaning."

"I can see that," says a cute Hispanic guy. "I'm Val."

"I'm Kylie. I hope this was okay."

"Sure," he says, coming down the hallway. "Knock yourself out."

I squint at him. "Actually, do you know anything about cleaning toilets? I mean, I understand the inside where the water is, but the outside...is there a special sponge for that or something?"

He turns around and eyes Brett, who's coming down the hallway behind him. "Is she serious?"

"Sounds like it," Brett says, and they both come into the bathroom, inspecting my work.

"I didn't want to use a towel," I say. "That seems unsanitary...for the towel."

Val leaves the room and Brett stands there looking at my phone propped up running a video of a woman mopping floors. "You have curious taste in porn. Is she gonna undress soon?"

I drop my head to the side. "It's instructional."

"You need instructions on mopping floors?"

"Clearly you do, as well, by the look of this place."

"I just moved in here last weekend."

I point at him. "So that's why Lauren thought this was an open spot. You'd just taken my place."

"No, I took my place." He looks at the toilet. "You do know the cleaner goes inside the bowl, right?"

"I put it in there."

"And everywhere."

"I'm trying, okay? Do you have any suggestions?"

He picks up the bottle and points to the spout. "That's why it's angled like this." He demonstrates for me, circling the rim of the bowl with the cleaner.

I put my hands on my hips. "That's not how she did it in the video."

He smirks at me. "You watched a video to figure out how to clean toilets, too? Do they not clean where you come from?"

Val shows up with a roll of paper towels. "Wet some of these and then wipe up the soap."

Brett snatches the roll from him and shoves it at his chest. "You wipe it up. It's your filth."

"Yours, too."

"I've just been here a week. This mold is yours from how long? A year? Two?"

Val purses his lips at us. "Fine. Get out. Both of you." Brett ushers me out.

"I really want to do this solo," I say. "I'm trying to say thank you for letting me stay."

"It's really not necessary."

"Well, if she's offering..." Val says.

"Shut up and clean your nastiness," Brett says.

"So damn bossy," Val says, unrolling some paper towels.

"What self-respecting gay man lives like this, anyway?" Brett asks.

"I break molds," Val says and then starts singing.

Brett closes the door behind him, leaving us standing in his bedroom. "I was actually just gonna go have breakfast with Tori."

"Oh, sure. Go."

"Did you wanna...come?" he asks.

As much as I would love to have breakfast, I don't have the funds. I'm looking at a pack of peanut butter crackers at best. "Nope. I'm cleaning this house."

He just stands there, staring at me. I can so easily see why these women around here fall for his charms. He's got this way of looking at me that makes me feel like I'm the only person on the planet...like I'm not the ditzy girl that my father and Josh have such a lack of respect for.

He lifts his eyebrows. "Do you mind if I change?"

"Oh," I say, coming back to earth. "Of course." I back out of the room, bouncing off the doorframe. He lifts his chin with that half smirk that I imagine has brought many women to their knees and then closes the door.

6

BRETT

"I thought you were spending today at your mom's," Tori asks, salting her eggs.

"I spent the night last night. Mimi needed some meds. Mom did some errands early this morning, but I'm going back tomorrow, too, just to give her a break."

"Will you be able to tear yourself away from the brunette bombshell staying at your house?"

I give her a look.

"What? You know you think she's hot. You could have invited her to come with us."

"I did," I say, forking a piece of my waffle. "She's cleaning the house."

She kicks me under the table. "Why aren't you helping her?"

"Ow. She said she wanted to do it solo."

"So? Your mom would kick your ass if she knew you were here stuffing your face when a stranger was home cleaning your house."

"Will you give me a break? I'm trying to figure this shit

out. She's staying with me this weekend. I need to keep space between us."

"What was up with you staking your claim on her with Jack last night, anyway?" Tori says, picking up her cup.

I know I was out of line putting my arm around her waist like that, but I don't want Jack anywhere near this girl. "So, you're cool if she gets with Jack?" I ask.

"This isn't about me. This is about you pissing on her like a dog marking his territory then pulling away."

I shift in my seat, my stomach full. "There's no need to get attached."

"She's a person, not a puppy. And she's our new co-worker."

"She's not working with us at Kids Company, is she?" I meet Tori's gaze.

"No."

Good. I'm drawn to this girl. I wouldn't want her in my workplace distracting me. "What job did she take here?"

Tori lifts an eyebrow. "You haven't asked her yourself?"

"Forget it," I say, taking a drink of my soda. I sit back, moving my plate toward the end of the table.

Tori gives me that look like she knows every inch of my brain, which is fair at this point in our lives. "Why do you have to always be such an ass to girls you like?"

I huff a laugh. "Girls I like. Who said I like this girl?"

"I say it."

"Why?"

"Because you didn't want Jack anywhere near her. You respect her," Tori says.

"That's ridiculous."

She lifts her eyebrows at me.

"You know what I mean."

She sits back, considering me. "Just be careful, there, Romeo."

"I'm not doing anything."

"We'll see about that. She's rich, you know."

"How do you know?" I ask, though I suspected the same thing. "I know she drives a luxury car, but if she's rich, why the hell is she staying with me and not in a hotel?"

"I'm talking about her family. Have you checked out her Insta?"

"Of course not." I don't dare tell her I tried but didn't want to request to follow her private account. "What were you doing checking her out?"

She gives me a guilty look. "Trying to figure out why in the hell she's starting work here as a pool attendant."

I blink my shock. "A pool attendant?"

"Yep."

I try to blow it off, but now I'm too interested. I assumed she was taking some cushy business office job. "What's in her Insta?"

She puts her fork down and pokes on her phone while she chews and then shows it to me. It's a picture of Kylie in a nice dress with a guy in a suit standing in front of what looks like a fancy hotel or a country club. My stomach groans. The greasy hash browns were definitely a mistake.

"That her boyfriend?" I ask, trying to sound unthreatened.

"I assume. Or an ex."

"What's the date on that post?" I ask.

She pulls her phone back to her chest, grinning at me. "You are into her."

I sit back, holding up both hands. "Fuck it."

"All I'm saying is be careful with this girl. There's something going on with her, and we don't know her or anything about where she comes from and who she's involved with."

"Got it," I say. "You done?"

She tosses her napkin on her plate. "Yep."

We pay, head to the car, and then ride in silence until I spot a bagel place and pull into the parking lot.

"Still hungry?" Tori asks.

"If she doesn't have enough money to stay in a hotel, I'm guessing she doesn't have a lot of money for food."

"There's a sucker born every day, isn't there?"

I put the truck in park. "A thank-you for cleaning the house. Don't you think my mom would approve of that kind of gesture?"

"Just as long as you're watching yourself. I get tired of doing that for you."

I glower at her as I get out of the car.

I DROP Tori off and then trod up the steps to my unit. When I open the door, the scent of cleaner has replaced the stench of sweaty feet. I find her in the kitchen putting a plate in the cabinet. She squints at me. "It's possible I may have rearranged some of your dishes, but not on purpose."

I hand her the bag. "I come with bagels."

She looks at it like it's a pot of gold. "You're kidding?"

"I wasn't sure which kind you'd like so I got some different ones."

She digs through the bag and looks up at me with almost weepy eyes. "There's cream cheese in here."

"I just got plain. There were too many flavors to choose from."

She throws her arms around me, hugging me to her like the end of it all is upon us. "Thank you."

I pull away before I get a big head. "It's just a bag of bagels."

"But it's..." She shakes her head, pinching the bridge of her nose like she's trying to think through emotions.

I want to ask her why a woman who drives a late-model luxury vehicle is tearing up over a bag of bagels, but I don't need to know the root of her problems. I'll just get sucked in. "Okay, well, I'm just gonna head to the beach. There's a spot where a lot of staff hang. It's right in front of the Dolphin's Fin...that's a restaurant, not an actual... Never mind." I head out the door, my heart pulling me back to the room like gravity taking hold, but I push through the pain and make it out the door without even so much as a beach towel.

7

BRETT

As expected, a group of my co-workers hang in our usual spot—hotties in bikinis batting off the dudes. This is what my weekends should look like. All is symmetrical with the world except the girl back at my house who won't get the hell off my brain.

Cohen stands at the shore watching his cousin Logan skid across the surf on his WaveRunner. I sidle up next to him. "Does he have buyer's remorse yet?"

"He will. I told him he'd be better off just renting one when he wanted to ride, but he wouldn't listen."

"He probably bought it to spite you."

Cohen eyes me like he hadn't thought of this option. "You're probably right."

Logan pulls into the shore. "What's up, OT? You wanna ride?"

I do, but I think I'm too antsy. I find myself checking the beach access stairs for some stupid reason...really stupid. "I'm good."

"Then let's play football." He shields his eyes from the

sun as he looks at the blankets where Bailey, Simone, and Isaac sit. "Isaac, you wanna play?"

"Sure," he says and hauls himself up. "Only if I can be on Cohen's team."

"No, fuck that," I say. "You and me."

"Why?" Isaac asks.

"Because if those two are on separate teams, they'll kill each other."

Cohen and Logan look at each other and shrug. They're cousins, but they're more like brothers with a vengeance for one another.

Logan tosses me the football, and we start a game. We're probably half an hour in when Tori strides toward the group with Kylie in tow. I hate that my stomach does that stupid fizzy thing when I see her.

"Dude," yells Isaac. "Eyes over here, man."

"Sorry," I say and make a point to play the game without looking at the blanket once, which takes some serious work on my part.

We finish the game and head over to the blankets, where Kylie has shed her cover-up to reveal a yellow sunflower bikini. Her brown hair drapes down her shoulders, and the sun brings out reddish highlights I didn't notice before. A smile stretches across her face as she talks to Bailey.

Kylie meets my gaze with a smile and then looks away quickly as something Bailey says gets her attention, and they laugh together. Damn, she's got a beautiful face when she laughs.

Logan and Cohen both collapse on the blanket while Isaac rifles through a cooler. I'm trying to figure out my next move when Kylie pushes herself up off the blanket. "I think I'm going to walk down the beach...check things out."

"I'll go with you," I say without even thinking about it, which earns me the side-eye from Tori.

As we head toward the shoreline, I say, "I see you're getting cozy with some of the girls."

"They're fantastic. I met Bailey and Simone last night. They're being super welcoming today."

"They're both sweet girls," I say.

She nods agreement and looks downward, twirling the string on the side of her bottoms. She's all torso in that bikini. Damn. "I wanted to tell you I'm sorry if I came on too strong in the kitchen. I wasn't trying to maul you, I promise."

I shrug as if I'm not even sure what she's talking about.

"I swear I'm not usually this emotional. It's been a rough few weeks."

"Want to tell me what happened?"

She rubs her forehead, thinking for a minute. "Let's just say I've been living with my head in the sand. I'm not used to being grateful for food. It's been an eye-opening experience."

I just nod, wondering what her story is, but I don't want to push her.

"I mean, I did a lot of charity work in my previous life, but I've never really understood what it's like to be totally on my own and literally hungry. I mean, usually I'm hungry on purpose because all women where I come from are hungry on purpose. But I've always known where my next gourmet salad or kale smoothie was coming from."

"What the hell's a kale smoothie? That sounds nasty."

"And that's not even fair for me to say," she says, ignoring my question. "I'm choosing to be on my own. If I got truly desperate, I do have...options." By the look on her face and the fact that she's sleeping in a stranger's bed for the weekend, I'm guessing the options aren't great. She glances over at me. "I know you probably want to roll your eyes at me."

"Not necessarily."

"It'd be okay if you did. I've been doing a lot of eye rolling at myself, lately."

I point at her. "I won't be peer pressured into an eye roll."

This gets a smile out of her, even though it's a small one. She heads into the water, so I follow her in. When we're both far enough out that we're past the breaking waves, she turns to me, waist-high in the water. "You Floridians have no idea how lucky you are. I've been landlocked for twenty-five years."

"You've been to the beach before this, though, right?"

"Yeah, but my crew usually goes to New York for shopping or to Sedona for spa treatments. My dad hates the beach. We always went to the mountains growing up. It made me a good skier, though."

"I am, too," I say.

She gives me a doubtful look. "Anyone can ski on the water. Try suiting up in a ton of garb and tackling the slopes in Aspen."

"You never had a boyfriend take you to Aruba or Cozumel?"

When the smile leaves her face, I want to kick myself in the nuts for pushing her. She gives a closed-mouth smile that doesn't reach her eyes. She turns and ventures out a little farther into the water, jumping waves, her mouth breaking out in a grin like she's ten years younger than she is. "This feels so good."

I join her, my body reflexively hopping waves with her like I haven't done since I was a kid. My mind goes to a memory from my childhood. Kylie looks at me curiously.

"What?" I say.

"It's just that I haven't seen you smile like this yet."

"Smile like what?"

"Like you've quit the player game for a second...like you genuinely mean it."

I turn away from her, embarrassed about how well she has my number. "I was just remembering something."

"Tell me about it."

I shake my head. "It's nothing really. Just a memory of Tori and me out here, each of us holding our little brothers as we jumped waves."

Kylie smiles so sincerely it makes my heart sore. "Tori's your family, isn't she?"

The idea strikes me as truer than anything I've ever known. "Yeah, I guess she is."

"Tell me about your brother."

A tornado of words and phrases collide in my brain when I think of Matthew. It's hard for me to put him or the need I feel to protect him into words.

"He's clever. Hates sports." I have to laugh at a memory. "I signed him up for this basketball league at the community center when he was six just to get us both out of the house. Other kids would toss him the ball and he would duck." I shake my head. "I had no idea what to do with him."

"What does he like to do?" she asks.

"He's into video games. It's always been a struggle, getting him to balance playing video games with going outside and doing stuff. But now he's interested in coding. So maybe some good can come out of his obsession after all." I try to keep a positive attitude about Matthew, but high school was no picnic, and now college is turning out to be an even bigger struggle for him.

"You sound like a father...a really good one, actually,"

she says with a smile that makes my stomach feel even looser than these waves.

I have to look away from her as my face heats up, and not from the sun. Nobody's ever given me that kind of validation when it comes to Matthew.

"I wish my father was as supportive as you are," she says with a smile that doesn't quite reach her eyes.

"What's going on with your dad?" I ask.

She turns toward the waves, her fingers skimming the water aimlessly. "He's just having a hard time digesting that he doesn't control me."

"You said your dad hates the beach. Is that why you came here?"

She huffs a laugh. "Probably. This was the first place that came to mind. My aunt brought me here once for vacation when I was about twelve. It was just the two of us. I loved it so much. We made sandcastles and walked on the beach every day. We worked puzzles at night and she showed me how to prepare seafood. It was the best week of my life. I guess when things went south, I wanted back in that world."

"Where is she now?" I ask.

She gives me half a smile. "She died a few years ago."

"I'm sorry."

She waves me off and lets out a strong exhale. "I guess we should head in before we shrivel up."

"Or the sharks start circling."

"Are there really sharks around here?"

"We are in the ocean." I focus on something behind her. "Shit, is that one?"

"Where?" she asks, grasping my arm.

I smile at her. "God, you're easy." She squeezes my arm, pursing her lips at me, and then we head in toward the shore. "Tell your dad you're sleeping in some guy's bed who you met yesterday. That'll piss him off."

She lifts her eyebrows. "For sure."

"Tell him I ride motocross, cage fight, and have a tattoo of a snake on my inner thigh."

"Is any of that true?" she asks.

"One of the three's true," I say, wanting to keep her guessing about me.

"Are you gonna tell me which one?"

"You'll have to find out."

We hold each other's gaze, and I start to wonder if she'd let me kiss her, when a wave breaks and she slams into me, the two of us going tumbling through the ocean, our slick bodies tangled up in one another's.

As we gather our footing, another one comes. "Crap. I guess I forgot what happens when you come into the breakers." She squints at the shoreline. "Wow, we're almost back where we started."

"That's the undertow. It pulls you in without you even knowing it's happening."

She looks away, unable to hide her smile, and I start to wonder what I'm getting myself into with her.

The ocean pushes us to the shore, and as we head over to the blanket, I see Tori sitting with the others, glancing between Kylie and me. Her gaze lands on me, and her eyes narrow. How that woman can make me feel like I'm inside out with one glowering look is beyond me.

Kylie collapses onto the blanket next to Simone and Bailey. Tori clears her throat, getting my attention. I mouth, *What?*

She lifts one eyebrow in that expert way she does, and I roll my eyes and sit at the other end of the blanket.

"What are we doing tonight?" Logan asks.

"Kylie here starts Monday at the lagoon pool," Bailey says. "Let's show her around in prep for her first day." Bailey's expression morphs into a sneaky smile.

"Hell yeah," Isaac says.

Simone flicks a bug off her knee. "We can't get her fired before she even starts. We like her." Simone smiles at Kylie, and Kylie grins back.

"Buddy's working security in that perimeter tonight," Bailey says.

"Ah," Simone says. "In that case, we're all clear. If everyone will pitch in ten, I'll make my famous margaritas."

"You've got to tell us what's in those," Cohen says.

"Never," Bailey says with a grin.

"I bet Jack Massey could get her to tell," Logan says and then ducks as Bailey throws her empty sparkling water can at him.

Tori shifts, looking at her phone like she's disinterested, but I know she never really got over him. I hate that he hurt her, and I hate worse that she can't seem to shake him.

Bailey stands and holds up her phone. "Venmo me, folks. Simone and I will head to the liquor store now."

"Done," Tori says, typing into her phone.

I pull out my phone and send her twenty. In a second, she looks up at me with a grateful smile. "Thanks, Brett."

"That's for her, too," I say, indicating Kylie. Tori gives me a raised eyebrow while I try to ignore her. "I'm going to eat if anyone wants to come," I say.

"I'll go," Cohen says.

Tori stands. "I'm gonna get a nap."

Logan nudges her. "I'm going with Tori." She shoves him and he stumbles backward with a grin. "Someday, sweetheart."

"In your dreams," Simone says. "I'm going with Bailey."

I glance at Kylie, who's getting to her feet. "You hungry?" I ask.

"No, I'm good. Are you okay with me going back to your place?"

"No problem. Val is probably gone to work now."

"He works on the weekends?"

"Yeah, caddies don't do the eight-to-five workweek."

"Sounds good," she says and then heads off.

We all scatter and Cohen comes up to me. "I've got my truck here. I'll drive."

"Cool." We head toward the parking lot.

"Did I fuck something up for you just then?" he asks.

I wave him off. "Hell no."

"She's cute."

"Mmm," I grunt.

Cohen chuckles.

"What?" I ask.

"It's just funny. Usually, when I say a girl's cute or hot, you're like, 'Yeah, she's bangable or whatever.'"

"I've never said bangable."

"You know what I mean."

"Fine, she's bangable. Happy?"

Cohen shakes his head. "Better watch out. Brett might be letting a girl get to him."

I go to push him, but he's already taken off, so I chase after him. But I'm downwind of the sand he's kicking up as he runs, so I finally give up.

8

KYLIE

I'm glad I made myself go to the beach. It gave me a chance to reconnect with some of the girls I met last night. I left with Bailey and Simone set up in my phone. I texted Bailey to send me her Venmo name, and she let me know that Brett covered my part, which makes me feel both guilty and giddy.

The best part of the day was getting to know him in the ocean. My stomach seesawed with the motion of the waves, and I can't be altogether sure his presence didn't add to that sensation.

I feel like there's so much more to him than the suave player he likes to make himself out to be. The genuine glimpses I get of him make me want to dig deeper.

I shower, dress, and then head to Bailey and Simone's unit, which is sort of catty-cornered from Brett's place. I'm glad to have the invitation so that I can get out of here before he returns home from going to eat with that guy Cohen, who was also super cute, by the way. What's in the water down here?

Bailey opens the door sporting a halter top bikini with a

mosaic print and a long, flowy skirt. I feel the closest to her of any of these women, mainly because she reminds me of one or two of the women in my circles back home. She's a fashionista, way more than I'd consider myself to be. I had a personal shopper in my former life. But I'm guessing her style is all her own. "Hey, girlie," she says. "Come on in."

We walk to the kitchen, where Simone is working on those margaritas that were promised. She's got on a black bikini and a red sheer skirt, both of which look stunning against her dark skin. Her braids are piled up in a bun on top of her head, showcasing her brown eyes. She hands me a plastic cup. "Tell me what you think."

I take a sip. "Wow, these really are good. What's the secret?"

Simone looks at Bailey as if she could be giving up the nuclear codes, and Bailey nods. "I think we're safe."

"Raspberry liqueur. Pretty simple, huh? But we've got the market on these things," Simone says.

"Yeah, we actually walked away with extra cash this time," Bailey says, smiling at Kylie. "I thought it was interesting that Brett covered for you. Is there a story there?"

Lord, is there. But I can't tell them my whole sordid mess...not right now, at least. I just want to have a fun night and pretend none of that happened at the moment.

"Definitely nothing going on there," I say.

"Are you sure?" Simone asks. "You two were pretty cozy out there in the ocean today."

Heat seeps up through my neck. "No, totally not. He's just helping me out this weekend."

"Helping you out how?" Simone asks.

I swallow before revealing my secret. "They screwed up my housing. They gave me the key to Brett and Val's place. I thought I was Val's new roommate."

"Did you deal with someone named Lauren in housing?" Bailey asks.

"How did you know?"

"She's been interning here for months. We've had so many complaints about her. We couldn't get her out of there fast enough, but it's a sticky relationship between the resort and the school she goes to. We had to grin and bear it until it was over. Needless to say, she was not offered full-time employment."

"So what happened?" Simone asks. "Did you let yourself into their apartment or something?"

"Oh, yeah," I say, starting to feel safe with these two. "I totally walked in on Brett. He had just gotten out of the shower," I say, a giggle getting the best of me, "and he was looking for a towel."

Bailey's eyes go wide. "You saw him?"

I nod, taking a sip of my margarita through a smile, that sense of giddiness taking over.

Simone lifts her eyebrows. "You've got to tell us. Are the rumors true?"

"Tell me what the rumors are first."

"They vary from he's hung like a horse to he has a snake tattoo on his inner thigh," Bailey says.

I can't help a smile. "I couldn't actually see his inner thigh, but I'm starting to wonder if that one might be true."

"And that other rumor?" Simone asks.

I think about Joshua standing next to Brett, and there's no contest. "That one might be true."

Simone gives the cutest laugh that makes me giggle with her.

"Well, I've definitely got him on my list of doable guys," Bailey says.

"Along with Jack Massey?" Simone asks.

This time, Bailey doesn't throw anything. "I wish everyone would just shut up about it," she says, but she smiles at her friend. Her expression turns serious. "Not that I could even if I wanted to."

Simone nods in agreement, taking a sip of her drink.

"That's right," I say. "You said you work in the business office, right? You must work with him or near him or whatever."

"That alone is reason enough," Bailey says.

"But not the only reason," Simone says, and the two of them give one another a knowing look.

"Is there a story here?" I ask.

"She wouldn't do it to Tori," Simone says.

"Ah," I say. "So it's Tori's story to tell."

"Not that you could get it out of her," Simone says.

"We both love her to death," Bailey says, "but she's got walls up the size of a skyscraper."

"So did they date?" I ask.

"For like five minutes," Simone says. "But it was an intense five minutes."

"Did Jack break Tori's heart?" I ask.

"Nobody's sure who broke whose heart," Simone says.

"I noticed he and Brett don't seem to get along," I say, instantly regretting it. I need to watch my gossip.

"I'm not sure that had anything to do with Tori," Bailey says. "They're both teacher's pet." Bailey and Simone exchange knowing looks again.

"What teacher?" I ask.

"Robert," Bailey says. "He's the guy who owns this place. He likes to pick someone to mentor every couple of years, usually a boy, of course. He'd been mentoring Brett for years when Jack came along. The two guys couldn't be more opposite if they tried. But both can't be favorite."

I have so many questions to ask, but I sip my drink, biting my tongue.

After about an hour of resort gossip and backstories on everyone we're going to meet, we head to the pool, dragging a wagon behind us with the margaritas in two big pitchers with spouts. We come in through an employee-only entrance, and I get my first look at my new workplace. It's definitely got an adults-only vibe. Rocky walls with waterfalls sprawl up the sides, and a large grotto you can swim in and out of sits at the top.

"They've got it going on here, don't they?" I say, taking it all in.

"Not your typical family resort," Bailey says. "Robert's goal is for this place to be an escape for parents. We've got an amazing pool for kids with all the slides and stuff and a lazy river ride on the other side of the resort, but this is where the adults come for sanity."

"My parents would have had us coming to this place when I was little if they'd known about it," Simone says. "God knows they needed some peace from my brothers and me."

"It's not open at nighttime?" I ask.

"It closes at seven," Bailey says. "Parents typically pick up their kids from Kids Company at five, so it's usually a ghost town here after that."

Bailey takes one side of the beverage dispenser and Simone gets the other. As they lift it onto the table, Simone says, "Lucky for us."

It's not long before the guys who were at the beach show up along with some others I don't recognize. I can't help it, but I scan each group as they come in the gate, hoping to see Brett, silly girl I am.

Bailey and Simone pull off their cover-ups, so I do the

same. I'm wrapped up in a conversation about office gossip led by Bailey when the gate clangs, and my attention is drawn to Brett, Tori, and Val. Tori is rocking a pair of cutoff jean shorts and a bikini top, working her curves like nobody's business. It seems impossible to me that Brett could not see her in a sexual way, but I remember that they are more family than anything.

Brett and Val take off their shirts and do matching flips into the pool.

"Show-offs," Bailey says, wiggling in her seat.

"Mmm-hmm," Simone says with a grin like she's got Bailey's number.

Drinks are poured, cans are popped, and everyone gets into the pool.

The girls minus Tori cluster at the three feet while the boys set up a basketball hoop that someone pulled from the employee-only area, and it's middle school all over again—boys versus girls on either side of the gym.

A security guard walks in and I think we're all sunk, but he just gets himself a margarita and leaves us. I turn to Bailey. "I see what you mean now. Lucky he's working, huh?"

"We wouldn't be here if he wasn't," she says with a waggle of her eyebrows.

Part of me feels like I'm back in college. I haven't done anything sneaky in eons. The pool parties I've attended in recent years have included high-end cocktails poured by a personal bartender and the latest theme in charcuterie boards.

The more drinks that flow, the closer the guys get to the girls. Flirtations start, and couples draw together like magnets.

Two of the guys I've met in the past couple of days approach our group. I'm still learning names, but I'm pretty sure the white guy is Logan, and the black guy is Isaac. "I'm walking over to the bar to get some ice," Logan says. "Y'all want to come? Sneak a shot while we're there?"

Bailey and Simone shrug and then turn to me. "You want to go?" Bailey asks.

I glance over at Brett, who is talking to Val and that other good-looking guy, Cohen, I think. He gives me that player smile he's so good at.

"I think I'll stay," I say.

The girls seem to catch on. "Cool," Bailey says.

"Come on, Kylie. I'll show you Big Fish Pub, my bar," Logan says.

Isaac backhands him. "The bar where he works."

"Same difference," Logan says with a smile. In fact, I'm not sure I've seen him without a smile on his face yet.

"I'll see it soon. I'm just gonna hang here and finish my drink."

"We'll be back in just a bit. It's right around the corner," Simone says.

"Take your time," I say.

They head out, and I relax back on the side of the pool, closing my eyes and letting my feet drift to the top of the water. I can feel movement toward me as the water pushes in my direction, and someone pinches my toe. I open my eyes to find Brett there, and my stomach does a little sizzle.

"What do you think about your new workplace?" he asks.

"If only I could hang out in the pool every day, this job would be fantastic."

"Better than working at the family pool, I guess."

"But I'm so good at picking up ice cream wrappers and shouting at kids to stop running."

"You may have to turn the hose on some couples in that grotto." He glances at it.

"Tonight?"

He grins. "Definitely, but during the week, too. The moms and dads start drinking about ten a.m. so they can sober up before they pick up their kids from us at five."

"That's what I hear. Sounds like a pretty good setup this resort has."

"You didn't want to go on a walk with the four of them?" he asks.

"And be a fifth wheel? How could I ever have turned that down?"

He smirks. "Simone and Bailey are good girls like you."

"Oh, yeah? And you know this how? Went there and got rejected?" The margaritas have fueled my engine.

He smiles that player grin that says he knows it all and I'm just a naïve little girl. "I didn't go there. I only hook up with women who aren't interested in more than the night ahead."

I nudge him in the stomach with my toe. "Because you're so above it all, aren't you?"

He grabs my foot, which is so strangely erotic. "I just like my freedom. You can't fault me for that."

"I'm enjoying my freedom." I tug my foot away from him before I get hot and bothered right here in this pool in front of God and everyone.

"Ten bucks says you left a boyfriend in Oklahoma."

I hold out my hand to him. "Pay up."

He gives me a skeptical look. "How do I know you're not lying to me?"

"Why would I lie?"

"Ten bucks."

"True, and I could use it right now, but it's no lie. I didn't leave a boyfriend there. I left an ex-boyfriend. Huge difference."

"I guess it is." He narrows his gaze at me. "Are you going to tell me the story?"

I turn away, biting the inside of my lip. "It's not my favorite subject."

"Then what is? Skiing?"

"Actually, I'd be happy to never go fucking skiing again in my life." The drink is definitely getting to me. I don't really cuss unless I'm drinking or really mad.

"Skiing equals boyfriend memories?"

I cup water in my hands, then watch it flow out, trying to avoid looking at him.

"Where is this asshole now?"

"Up my dad's butt, I suppose."

"So he got your dad in the breakup?"

"He can have my dad. I'm not interested in a father who takes his daughter's cheating fiancé's side over hers." My stomach sours with the swirl of the drink and the betrayal of my father.

He lifts his eyebrows. "Fiancé, huh? Now you've got to tell me the rest of the story."

I pick up my cup. "Margaritas cause loose lips."

"Nah, they just help you get out all the bullshit inside that's erupting."

I consider him, wondering if he's really interested or if he's humoring me. "So you're saying if I unburden myself to you now, I'll feel better?"

"Guaranteed. And the best part about it is you know I'll never tell anyone."

"How do I know that?"

"Because I'm loyal." The intense look in his eyes makes me believe him.

"Guaranteed, huh?"

He crosses his heart, not breaking his gaze from mine.

I'm just tipsy and desperate enough to take him up on his offer, even if he's only humoring me...or trying to soften me up so I'll hook up with him later. "I walked in on my fiancé in bed with another woman."

He winces. "That's tough."

"Yep."

"Where were they...in your bed?"

"Well, technically, it was his bed. I hadn't officially moved in yet. I was still living at my dad's house." I hold up a hand. "I know a person in her mid-twenties should have her own place, for the record."

"I just moved out from my mom's place last week."

"Really? Like for the first time?"

He nods. "Keep going."

"The whole thing was particularly painful because he and I had given up on foreplay years ago, and the two them were engaged in..." I make a motion with my hand.

"Oral?"

I scratch my neck, hoping my face isn't candy-apple red. "Mmm-hmm."

"Why had you given up on foreplay?"

I mess with my eyebrow, hoping to cover my eyes. "That should have probably been my first sign, right?"

"Would have been mine. So what happened?"

"I had a whole speech prepared, but I chickened out and bolted."

"You knew you were going to find them?"

"I was clued in by a friend...my only friend." I try to put everyone close to me who kept it from me out of my brain.

"Who was the woman?"

"She was one of our friends...or his friends, I should say. I thought she was my friend."

"That's shitty."

I nod, trying not to let it all come flooding in again, but it's hard to keep the memories at bay. "We were all friends—this group of us, like five couples. We hung at each other's houses all the time. Those New York shopping trips I mentioned earlier today? She was a part of those. She was a part of everything."

"And the whole time, she was with him?"

"Yeah. I'm like, why not just go be together? She's married, but she and her husband don't have kids or anything." I go to take a drink from my cup, but it's empty.

"Are they together now?"

"I don't know, and I don't care," I say, realizing that statement is becoming true.

"What about your ex? How's he handling you leaving?"

I inhale a deep breath. "I don't know. He keeps texting. I get the feeling he thinks this is just a little bump in the road."

"How do you feel?"

I think carefully before responding, wanting to make sure I get my wording correct, not only for Brett's sake but for my own. "Relieved."

He lifts his eyebrows, waiting for me to elaborate, but I'm not sure I want to get into the rest right now. I duck under the water, unable to take the humiliation anymore. While I'm under there, the degradation of five years of bullshit hits a crescendo, and something inside of me snaps.

9

BRETT

When Kylie emerges from the water, she closes the distance between us. I hold my position steady, but I have to admit, she's throwing me off guard.

Smoothing her dripping hair out of her face, she says, "What's wrong, super stud?"

I try not to chuckle at her choice of wording. Sometimes she's like a girl from a different era...like she's been in a storm shelter for fifty years and was just recently released. Hmm, she is from Oklahoma...

She flicks me on the shoulder. "You like being the one to make the moves, don't you? You like being the cat who chases the skunk."

"Excuse me?" I ask.

"You don't know Pepé Le Pew?"

"Pepper what?"

"From *Bugs Bunny*."

"I know *Bugs Bunny*," I say, remembering watching it on that classic cartoon channel. "Matthew loved Speedy Gonzalez."

She points at me. "That's me. Speedy Gonzalez, running from you, the skunk."

I lift my chin. "Who said I was chasing anything?"

"That's what I thought," she says, giving me a little splash.

"Are you drunk?" I ask, because I really can't tell if she is or not.

She runs her finger through the water. "I'm fluffy. There's a big difference between drunk and fluffy."

This makes me grin. "Oh, yeah? What's the difference?"

"If I were drunk, I couldn't do this."

She goes underwater and stands on her hands, holding the position steady. I can't help myself, so I grab her ankles and tug her body up. She parts her legs and somehow they get wrapped around my waist. I'm honestly not sure if I did it or if she did, but either way, it feels good to have them bound around me. She comes up out of the water, laughing as her legs tighten their grip on my waist.

I can't help laughing with her. "Definitely drunk," I say as a tease. I'm not sure a drunk person could have held that handstand like she did.

"I'm not," she says, resting her hands on my shoulders. "I'm just enjoying myself." She gazes into my eyes and it's so tough to read her. She's not over-the-top flirty like the other girls I'm usually with who give me those unmistakable fuck-me eyes. She genuinely seems to just be having a good time. She hops down off of me and goes over to the side of the pool, checking her cup. "I've only had two margaritas. I'd have to be a super lightweight to get drunk off that."

I run her words from a few minutes back through my head and flick some water at her. "What did you mean by *that's what I thought*?" I say.

She finally gives up on her cup and leans against the

side of the pool. "You talk a big game, flirting and making these vague suggestions to me, but I bet you anything if I were to pull you into your bed with me tonight, you'd go all gentlemanly on me."

I have to laugh, the word being so absurd. "Would not."

"Oh, yes, you would. You're terrible at this whole bad-boy thing."

"Bad boy," I say, shaking my head. I lean back on the side of the pool like I own the place, playing up to this role she's created for me. Why the fuck not.

"I know your kind," she says. "Just enough edge to you to make the girls pant. You want them to think you don't care, but you care."

I roll my eyes at her, shaking my head like she's full of nonsense.

"If you didn't care, you wouldn't be sleeping on your couch. You'd be making me sleep there."

"Who says I slept on the couch? You don't know where I slept last night."

"I know you'd love me to think you had some amazing threesome or something. But I know you were probably out helping some old lady cross the street."

"That would take me all night?"

She gauges me. "You were prepping food in a soup kitchen or making repairs on an old house for someone... building schools for underserved communities."

"I'm sorry to crush your image of me, but I've never done any of those things."

She points at me. "But you did help a homeless girl who had nowhere to stay. Don't even try to deny it."

"I told a hot girl she could sleep in my bed. I'm hardly expecting the medal of honor."

She smiles at me as she runs her fingers through the water, making little waves.

If this were any other girl, I'd already be in bed with her, but the fact that I'm having more fun than I should right now is a red flag to me that I need to pull back. "Besides, you're off-limits to me. I couldn't even hook up with you if I wanted to."

"If you wanted to, huh?" she says.

"Yeah, *if* I wanted to."

"And why's that?"

"Because I work with you."

She glances around the pool at the people who've paired up, several couples—even a threesome looking like it's getting underway. Damn, this group is like a bunch of rabbits in heat.

"Yeah, because nobody breaks that rule, do they?" She peers around the pool. "What's going on over there in that grotto?"

She doesn't give me a chance to answer, just ducks under the water and swims that way, her long legs pushing through the water, her hair loose around her like a mermaid. I try letting her go and not following, but as she peers into the grotto and then looks at me with wide eyes, dropping her jaw, I can't help wanting to be with her as she discovers the place for the first time.

I wade over there and take it in from her view—low lighting giving off an intimate vibe, small waves lapping the steps leading up to the hot tub, the strategically placed privacy cubbies.

She wades in farther. "I thought this was a family resort."

"It is, but Robert knows that the moms and dads are the ones making the decisions about where they vacation each year. So he makes it where they want to come back as much as their kids do."

She meets my gaze. "Robert's the guy who owns this place, right?"

"Yeah," I say. I guess I assumed she'd know that.

She stares at me like she's thinking about asking me something personal, but then she just glances around the grotto again. "I'm surprised this place closes at seven. It seems like such a nighttime vibe."

I pick up a beach ball that's floated my way and knock it across the pool. "You'd be surprised. The moms and dads spend their days at this pool. This place makes them feel like different people. It's an escape."

She nods, glancing around. "Nice. So you and Tori work with their kids while they come here?"

"Us and some others. Simone's our physical therapist."

"She mentioned that." Her lips quirk up in a small smile. "I bet you all have a lot of patience."

"You have to have patience when you're working with kids."

She walks up the stairs to the hot tub. "So you're an occupational therapist for kids, and you're telling me you're a bad boy?"

"I'm sure I didn't say I was a bad boy."

She dips a toe in the water. "What's the correct term then, player? Hookup king?"

I roll my eyes. "This is getting old," I say, but I'm not one bit tired of her.

She sits on the edge of the hot tub, letting her feet dangle in. "You never did tell me how you got into occupational therapy for kids. I mean, I know you worked in games and then moved to Kids Company. But why OT?"

I walk up the stairs and sit near her, careful not to get too close. I don't like talking about Matthew to strangers, but she opened up to me, and that couldn't have been easy. I guess it wouldn't hurt to share a little. "That was more out of necessity than anything."

"What kind of necessity?"

I scratch my forehead, my chest panging, but she's not some girl I'm gonna sleep with then move on from. She seems like she might actually care about what I've got to say. "I knew someone who could use the help."

She considers me. "Your brother?"

I'm surprised that she put it together, but then I remember telling her a little about Matthew in the ocean earlier. I look down at my hands and nod.

"Does your brother have a diagnosis?"

I huff a laugh. "Diagnoses are for kids with families who have money, or at least have their kids in schools with money. The school my brother and I went to struggled just to feed all the kids." I get the feeling she never looked for her next meal to be provided by the school.

She blinks. "I thought pretty much all schools in the United States were required to offer help for kids with special needs."

"Ours did, but our schools were so underfunded, unless there's an obvious need, you really have to have someone to advocate for you. I was fourteen when Matthew was seven. I was never even in the same school as he was. I had no idea anything was really wrong until a teacher came to our house one day to talk to my mom about it all."

"That seems unusual—a teacher coming to your house."

I don't want to badmouth my mother, so I just say, "It was an unusual situation. Of course, it did no good. My mom was dating this worthless dickhead at the time, and he told the woman to stay out of our business. That was the end of that." The memory has me gritting my teeth.

I dare a glance at her, and the look of pure heartbreak in her gaze makes my stomach roll. I shake it off and hop into the hot tub. "Fuck it." I hold my hand out to her. "Come on in. The water feels good." Reluctantly, she takes my hand, and I pull her in. "Did I lie?"

She cups water with either hand and lets it drain into the tub. "You did not."

I meet her gaze, letting my hand brush hers. She doesn't move it, so I take it in mine, my instincts working harder than my willpower. She's lost her bravado, becoming shy and tentative. This is the moment I should pull her to me, taking charge of this situation and getting her to give herself to me for the night.

"Hot tub time!" comes a shout from the opening of the grotto, where Simone, Bailey, Logan, and Isaac crash the moment, wading toward us. Kylie and I pull away as they all infiltrate the hot tub with stories from their walk...something about catching Buddy taking a whizz behind a bush, an image that definitely breaks the mood I had going with Kylie. It's probably for the best, because if I were to have taken her to bed tonight, I'm not sure I could have walked away tomorrow.

10

KYLIE

I wake up around ten, but the house is still quiet, so I brush my teeth, get dressed, and then head for the front door. Unlike yesterday morning, Brett is asleep on the couch...or at least he's pretending to be.

I try not to stare for too long, but it's really hard. I feel like we turned a corner last night. I think he might have been getting ready to kiss me when the group came back from their walk. And I'm pretty sure I would have let him, silly girl I am. It's so like me to be a pawn in the playbook of the first player I meet post-breakup.

I walk to the business center, taking in the resort for the first time in the daylight. A family crosses the street loaded down with bags and pool noodles, headed toward the large pool with the lazy river ride and slides. I pass the golf club where men in polos and khaki shorts walk toward the entrance hauling sets of clubs over their shoulders. Around the corner, women in expensive tennis skirts and tanks sweat it out on the court in a doubles match, giving me a touch of nostalgia for my old life. As I remember the deception and betrayal of the women I played tennis with, I'm jerked back to reality, ready to plow forward and get this online orientation done.

I set up my laptop in the business center. I stupidly assumed this would be a short video I could watch at some point during my first week, but after reading through my welcome email to see where I needed to report in the morning, I realized this orientation was a bigger deal than I thought. Apparently, they don't trust that you'll watch the video on your own, so there's a test at the end of it. I tried taking the test after watching the first ten minutes of the video, and I failed it, miserably.

Two hours later, I'm still trying to get this thing finished. You have to take the test until you get it perfect, and I can't get it right. Part of my problem could be that I keep drifting off during the video, thinking about Brett's lips and the touch of his hand on mine in the hot tub last night.

"Hey," comes a guy's voice. I look up to find Jack Massey standing there in gym shorts and a T-shirt.

I sit back. "Hey," I say, giving him a smile. There's something comforting about Jack. He definitely reminds me of guys I've been around my whole life. While Brett is mysterious and all bad boyish, Jack is like my favorite blanket.

"You do not look happy," he says.

"I'm just having trouble with this orientation video. What are you doing here?" I ask, glancing around the place.

"I can't keep away from the office. It's connected through that lobby," he says, pointing behind me. "What's going on with the video?" he asks, sitting down beside me.

"It's working fine. Operator error," I say. "I'm having focus issues, I guess."

"How can that be possible with the stimulating material in that thing?"

I smile at him, rolling my eyes at myself.

He points to my laptop. "May I?"

"Sure," I say.

He flies through the test, hitting answers and arrowing through like a machine. I glance around, trying to be cool about this, but I've never cheated on anything in my life. He reaches the end of the test and the words *Congratulations, you passed!* fill the screen, and relief floods my chest. "You've saved my life."

He hands me the computer back. "It's pretty easy when you're the one who came up with the questions."

"So I can blame you for this?"

"Sorry, Robert said to make it tough. He wants people to take it seriously."

"Now I feel guilty."

"Don't. You've been working on this thing for like two hours."

I shift my body to face his. "How do you know that?"

"I get an alert when a new hire logs into the test."

I frown at him. "So you knew I was here this whole time?"

"Pretty much."

I consider him. "Did you come here just to help me with this?"

He shrugs. "I went and lifted some weights first. When I never got the notification that you passed, I thought I'd come check on you."

I smile at him. "So you do this for all the new hires?"

"Oh, hell no."

This makes me giggle, and then I straighten up. "I guess I'm really working that damsel-in-distress angle this weekend."

"Maybe I just wanted to say hi," he says. I can't tell if he's flirting or just trying to be my friend.

I look down at my laptop to avoid his gaze. "I heard some stories about you this weekend."

"Oh, yeah?" he says.

"Mmm. The words *teacher's pet* were used."

He raises his eyebrows. "Hargrove said that about me? That's a bit hypocritical."

"No, it wasn't him. I was hanging out with some girls I met who work here."

"Ah. Well, I can't really deny it. Robert's been mentoring me since I was a junior in college. He came to Cornell to speak about resorts that are thinking outside the box, and I was so impressed with him I waited a half hour to meet him. We stayed in touch, and he offered me an internship. I've been working for him ever since."

"So he mentored both you and Brett at the same time?"

"Hargrove's story is a bit different from mine. He's been working with Robert since he was sixteen."

"He mentioned that. He was working in games and then got interested in Kids Company."

"He was interested in Kids Company before he ever came to work here." He looks at me and then shakes his head. "Sorry. Not my story to tell."

"Because of his brother," I say, putting together that it was no accident that he happened upon Kids Company. My heart constricts as I think of him as a teenager trying to help his brother when the school system failed him.

Jack narrows his gaze. "Yeah. I'm surprised he opened up to you about Matthew. Brett gets pissed if anyone even mentions his brother." He huffs a laugh. "Damn, you hooked him fast."

"It's not like that. We're totally platonic," I say, my neck sizzling.

"You might be. He's not if he's talking to you about his brother."

I shift in my seat, tucking a lock of hair behind my ear, not sure what to say.

"Robert took Brett under his wing because he appreciated his dedication to his brother and his tenacity to find this resort and get a job here doing whatever he could just to get his brother help. Services are free to family members of employees. Robert took me under his wing because of my detachment from my family and my ability to be cutthroat in business."

"I guess the two of you really are opposites."

He gives me a humorless smile. "Yeah, but I'm the stupid one. If I wanted a chance with you, I wouldn't have told you what a great guy Hargrove is despite his façade."

His words come off self-deprecating, but his bravado tells a very different story. I'd bet my last precious dollars he never had any intention of asking me out. "You didn't have to tell me Brett's a good guy underneath his act. I figured it out for myself."

"Not surprised." He stands. "But do watch yourself. He's broken more hearts around here than questions on that stupid test." He holds up a hand in a wave as he walks away.

I close my laptop and pack up, my stomach growling as I head out. I can't get Jack's words out of my head. I don't want to be that girl who thinks she's the exception. Sure, Brett and I have had some good conversations, but that doesn't mean I'm special. He breaks hearts. That's what he does, good guy or not. The last thing I need right now is more harm to my already damaged heart.

11

KYLIE

I make it home...I mean back to Brett's house, by five thirty. The fumes of disinfectant are replaced by sizzling meats, onions, and peppers. I haven't had anything to eat today besides a pack of crackers this morning and a candy bar for a consolation prize after I failed the test for the second time. I'm so hungry I could eat my hand.

I peer into the kitchen to find Brett in there with a spatula. "You cook?" I ask.

He glances over at me, giving me that cool guy smile. "When I'm hungry."

I walk in and pick up a chip from a bowl of them. "Wow, you really can cook. This is a lot," I say, looking at the tortillas, bowls of shredded cheese, salsa, guacamole, and a pan of pinto beans on the stove.

"Tori and I try to do a family dinner about once a month. She'll be over in a minute."

"Ah," I say, feeling a tad dejected, which is silly. It's not like he'd done this for me...of course.

"Where have you been today?" he asks, not looking at me.

"Orientation, online."

"I've heard that test is rough. Did you pass?" He meets my gaze, and I'm tossed back into last night when he held my hand in the pool, and I find myself looking away, afraid he can read my thoughts.

"I did, but I had a little help." I inwardly wince after saying it. I don't want to get Jack in trouble.

"Who from?" he asks, looking suspicious.

"Doesn't matter."

He looks down at the skillet with a snide smile. I guess I'm not nearly as good of an avoider as I thought I was.

My stomach gives off a loud growl, and he lifts his eyebrow, looking at it.

"Sorry," I say, putting a hand over it.

"We'll probably eat around seven. Drinks as soon as Tori gets here with the sangria and beer."

I give an indifferent nod, though I'm doing cartwheels on the inside. "Great," I say, and then skedaddle down the hallway to his room.

I jump in the shower and then dress, putting on just enough makeup to not be able to tell I have any on. I squirt one quick pump of my body mist into the air and walk through it and then let out a sigh, giving myself a last check. *More broken hearts than questions on that test.* There were fifty questions on the test. That's a lot of broken hearts.

When I get back to the kitchen, the small space is packed. Tori holds a pitcher of red liquid with fruit soaking in it, and she pours it into clear plastic cups on the counter. A couple I don't know flirt over the guacamole. The girl dips a chip and tries to feed it to the guy. "You sure you want me to have onions? Because we're gonna be doing some making up later on this evening," he says, snaking his arms around her waist.

"I've got you a toothbrush," she says.

"You didn't throw it out after last week?"

She gives him a playful grin. "You know I didn't."

"Kylie," Tori says, getting everyone's attention, "that sickening display is Janelle and Chris."

Janelle has backed into Chris, and he has his arm around her waist. "It's nice to meet you," he says with a smile the size of Florida. He's definitely cute.

"Hi." I turn to Janelle. "You're Tori's roommate?"

"I am," she says, her smile matching his. Yep, major make-up sex happening on this street tonight.

"Where do you work in the resort?" I ask.

"I'm in marketing and PR," Janelle says. "It's my job to make this place look even better online than it does in person."

Chris reaches down to her ear. "They just need to post pictures of you on the website and they'd have this place at capacity year-round." He's right about that. She's got big, beautiful eyes like Issa Rae. He bites her earlobe, and she wiggles away from him with a grin. Their chemistry together is so hot I think I might need another shower...a cold one.

"You must work with Bailey," I say to Janelle.

"Yep. Partners in PR crime."

I smile and turn to Chris. "What do you do?"

He takes a chip. "I don't work here. I'm at the hospital."

"Nice. What do you do there?"

"Accounting."

"Who wants sangria?" Tori asks, passing cups out. Chris and Janelle both take one. Tori picks up two more cups and hands one to Brett, proffering the other toward me. I feel guilty for not contributing to the evening. Back home, I would have brought a pricey bottle of wine. But I don't even have the money for a low-dollar bottle at this point. "Kylie?" Tori asks, nodding at the drink.

"Thanks," I say, taking it, swallowing my guilt and humility. At times like this I feel like a fraud...like if these people saw where I moved here from and the extravagant habits I left behind, they wouldn't be so accommodating.

Tori picks up the final cup and holds it up to the group. "To fajita night."

"To fajita night," we all say in unison and then sip our drinks.

I'm aware of the front door opening, and then Val appears in the kitchen with a twelve-pack of imported beer. "Pardon me, pretty ladies."

"Who are you calling a lady?" Chris asks.

Val puckers up and makes a smooching sound in Chris's direction, and he ducks away from him. Val puts the beer up and then faces me. "I owe you. This place looks fantastic."

"She takes Venmo," Janelle says.

"Oh, shit, sure," Val says, pulling his phone out of his pocket.

I open my mouth to protest, but the idea of actually receiving some money is too tantalizing.

Brett hands me some bills. "Here. I got this when I went to the store earlier today. Thanks for cleaning."

I shake my head, eyeing the cash like it's a glass of ice water in the middle of the Sahara.

"Girl, take that money," Janelle says. "You earned it if you cleaned this nasty-ass pit."

Brett slides the cash into my pocket, and I'm too mesmerized by his eye contact to argue.

Tori picks up the bowl of chips. "Let's move this into the

dining room. We're gonna all get pregnant if we get any closer in this kitchen."

"Let's have a drink before we eat," Val says. "It'll be too hard to catch a buzz otherwise."

"True," Chris says, taking a long drink of his sangria.

I follow the group into the living room, and as Brett comes in, he looks at me with that grin that hides so much.

"I didn't know you could be so domesticated," I say.

He chuckles. "That's the last word anyone's ever used to describe me."

"Seriously, look at you. You're throwing a dinner party."

"It's not a dinner party. It's me making dinner and all you people eating it."

I point at him, squinting. "I think that might be a dinner party." I hold my cup up to his. We knock them together and then take drinks, both keeping an eye on one another.

Someone has turned on music, which seeps from a speaker positioned next to the television, and Janelle and Chris dance like we're in a club. Tori looks like she's feeling good, moving to the music and sipping her drink while Val moves up to her.

I look at Brett, because we're the only two idiots not dancing, but I'm absolutely rotten at it. I've never felt the music in my bones to the point of moving my body, not since I was a toddler and didn't care what anyone thought. I've never felt like a sexpot a day in my life, and today is no exception.

Brett takes my hand and twirls me slowly, and I like that I don't have to duck. Joshua was a little shorter than me, which I never minded, but it's nice to be face-to-face with a guy who's a little taller than me.

The song ends, and everyone breaks apart for a moment, but the next song that starts is this Sofi Tukker song that I love, and I jump with excitement, splashing a little sangria out of my cup. "Oh, crap!"

Brett chuckles. "I doubt that's the worst that's been on this floor." He sets my cup down on the dining room table along with his, then takes my hands in his and pulls me into an open space in the living room. Someone turns the music up, and before I know it, we're full-on dancing together like Tori and Val and Janelle and Chris. Well, not exactly like Janelle and Chris. They may be headed toward an R rating. But we are dancing, and I'm letting loose and moving like I'm a totally normal person who has been dancing in the clubs for years and not spending weekends at posh restaurant openings and snooty wine bars. Brett and I have our fingers threaded together, and we move close then pull away and tease and taunt, and it's so freaking fun.

A knock sounds at the door, and Val opens it. Some people from last night, including Bailey and Simone, come in. We hug like it's been years since we've connected. They make a sandwich out of me before I even know what's happening. I have never been a girl who's danced like this with other girls, but something about this is okay with me. If my circle of friends back home could only see me now, they'd all be clutching their pearls.

I don't know how many songs I've danced to or how many people I've danced with, but this has become a full-on party. At some point, Brett handed me my drink, which I drank. At another point, someone handed me a shot, which I did, and now I'm just fluffy enough that I either need to eat or pass out somewhere. I'm not a lightweight, but the lack of food is definitely a problem.

I glance around for Brett and find him right behind me. I tug on his shirt, and he leans in toward me. "I've got to eat or pass out."

"Come on," he says, and I follow him into the kitchen.

He opens a drawer and pulls out two forks, and then he picks up one of the pans. "Grab those," he says, motioning to the flour tortillas.

I take them and follow him as he maneuvers through the crowd to his bedroom and shuts and locks the door behind us. We collapse onto the bed, and he pulls the lid off the pan.

"Oh, my God. Cold meat has never looked so amazing," I say.

He hands me a fork, and we dig in like savages. I eat what feels like half the pan before I pull a tortilla out of the bag. "I haven't unabashedly eaten carbs without analysis and justification in at least half a decade." I offer the bag to him. "You want one?"

"Mmm-hmm," he says and takes it from me and rips it in half with his teeth like a dog. We both crack up so hard that we're doubled over when someone bangs on the door. "Brett, are you in there?" some guy shouts.

"Fuck off. I'm trying to get laid," Brett shouts back, which has us laughing even harder. We both hold our fingers over our mouths, instructing the other one to "Shhhhhhhh."

We fall on our backs from laughter and full bellies. He moves the pan to the floor and then lies back with his hands behind his head. "That was fun."

"Mmm-hmm," I utter. "I haven't eaten like that in years... maybe since college."

He eyes me, looking so freaking sexy with the muscles in his triceps bulging. "Where do you come from?" he asks.

I look at him over my shoulder. "Oklahoma."

"I don't mean where in the country. Who were your people? What was your world like before this?"

I exhale a deep breath and lie back on the bed, resting

my head in my hand. "You don't wanna know. It's super boring."

"I'm interested. You seem like a fish out of water here."

"Why do you say that?" I ask, though it could be one of many things, including my BMW that I expect to disappear any day now when my dad figures out where I am and that I'm not coming back, or my dance moves, which scream of my lack of clubbing experience.

"Things like eating a tortilla seem like a new experience for you."

"Ah. The tortilla gave me away, huh?"

He rolls over onto his side, facing me, sliding his arm under his pillow. "Not just the tortilla. You seemed to really enjoy yourself tonight...like maybe you haven't in a while."

I can't help a smile. "I'm having a ball. My circle of friends doesn't cut loose like this."

"This is the same group who didn't tell you your fiancé was cheating on you?"

"Those are the ones. If we went clubbing, it was to some VIP lounge somewhere. And no one dared to dance...not like that, at least."

"What did you do with your days in this other life?"

I hide my face in the pillow. "I was hoping to avoid that question."

"How come?"

"Because it's embarrassing," I say, rolling onto my side.

He just stares at me, willing me to speak like he's controlling my mind with his hotness.

"I didn't really have an official job. I mean, I worked for my dad's company, in a way. I planned all their parties, fundraisers, retirement celebrations. I did do charity work, but not enough."

"Walk me through a typical day. You wake up and..."

I close my eyes. "This is so embarrassing."

"It was your life. You shouldn't be ashamed of it."

"But I am, at least around you and your friends. You're all hardworking, respectable people. I've been floating through life with oblivious abandon. Look where it got me."

He just stares at me, his gaze focused on me, giving me his full attention. I can't remember the last time Joshua really listened to me about anything.

"I would wake up and get dressed and go get a juice or something. Then I'd go to Pilates or yoga. I always got that out of the way early."

"What's early?"

I wince. "Like, ten?"

He just nods.

"Then I'd shower, and if I didn't have an appointment for my hair or nails or a spa treatment of some kind or lunch scheduled with a friend, I'd stop in at my dad's office and sort of do the rounds."

He smiles. "What were the rounds?"

I flick him in the chest. "You're judging me."

"I'm not. Go on."

Even though revealing the details about the life I just left sucks, it does feel a bit like coming clean. "I would get platters of cookies from the bakery and leave them in the different departments, or I would see if anyone needed anything for their office...picture frame for their kid's new school photo, vase of fresh flowers for the conference room. Sometimes I'd get coffee orders for a certain department that I knew was working on a big project...that sort of thing."

"Sounds like a generous way to spend your time."

I scratch my eyebrow, my stomach sizzling a little. "Well, to be fair, it wasn't my money. I had a corporate card."

"Still. It sounds like you enjoyed taking care of people."

I shrug. "I guess I did. I do. But now all of you are taking care of me. It's...humbling." I bite back the urge to tear up.

"I assume you don't have that corporate card anymore?"

I shake my head, falling onto my back. "I don't have any of my credit cards anymore. It was a whole thing."

"What kind of thing?"

"When I found out about Joshua cheating, I told my dad, thinking he'd be outraged on my behalf. But he handled me like I was overreacting. I knew my dad had cheated on my mom. That was no secret. But I didn't think he'd be okay with me being treated that way."

"What happened?"

"I told him the wedding was off and that I was breaking up with Joshua. At first, he was kind and understanding about it, saying I just needed to cool off. But after a few weeks, when I still wouldn't see Joshua, he had this talk with me about it. I told him I was done, and he asked me to reconsider. When I said no, he got forceful with me."

"Like threatening?" Brett asks, looking concerned.

"Not physically, of course. But he made it clear he would cut me off if I didn't take Joshua back." The sting of my dad's betrayal numbs me once again.

"Why?"

"You've got to understand my dad. Joshua and he are thick as thieves. He's been grooming Joshua for years, ever since he and I started dating. My dad's invested in him—both time and money. Joshua went to grad school on the company's dime. My dad's plan was for me to marry Joshua and him to run the business in a few years when my dad's ready to retire. My breaking up our relationship tosses a huge kink in his plans."

"So your dad's just okay with you being with a guy who cheats on you?"

"Like I said, he cheated on my mom, constantly. To him, that's just what men do."

"Yeah, but to cut you off is a big deal, isn't it?"

"To me, of course, but I'm sure he thought just the threat of cutting me off would be enough to make me change my mind. I think I've rattled him, forcing him to make good on his threat."

He quirks a smile at me. "That's kind of badass."

I shrug, accepting the win, no matter how small.

"Do you think he'll give in?" he asks.

"You don't know my dad. He's never given in a day in his life. Everyone's always talked about how ruthless he is in business. I never thought I'd be on the other end of his gun, but here I am." The hole in my chest deepens.

"You've never crossed him before?"

"Not really. Not where it counted. There's a lot at play here. He wants to avoid the scandal of it all. Everyone was super involved in our relationship...always asking why we hadn't gotten married already so we could start pumping out babies right away."

"Why hadn't you? Was one of you holding out?"

I purse my lips at him, running my fingers along the trim of the blanket. "Yeah, me."

He lifts his eyebrows.

"My aunt I was telling you about...she'd made me promise that I wouldn't get engaged until I was twenty-five. She talked a lot about the frontal lobe and how it wasn't fully developed until that age and that no young person should make any important decisions until after it was done developing. I think it was just her way of delaying the inevitable. She never liked Joshua. She never liked my dad, either, for that matter."

He just gazes at me, his eyelids getting heavier.

"I'm sorry. I've gone on and on here."

"I'm interested. I want to hear it."

"I want to forget about it."

He pulls me into his chest, and the warmth of his body and the touch of his hand against my back loosen my burden, even if it's temporary.

"I'm just gonna rest my eyes a minute," he says. "When they all leave, I'll move to the couch, okay?" he says, his words a little slurry.

"Mmm-hmm," I utter and close my eyes, allowing myself to give in to the luxury of him.

12

KYLIE

"Kylie." My name is a low grumble in a dreamy space.

"Hmm," I manage to get out in my fuzzy state.

A hand squeezes my shoulder. "Kylie, it's Monday. It's almost nine."

A jolt shocks me fully awake, and I'm off Brett's chest, where apparently I've been all night long. Memories of dancing, tequila shots, and cold meat flood into my brain.

"Crap," I say, glancing around. "I'm supposed to be at the lagoon pool at nine."

"I'll drop you over there."

I pull myself off the bed and glance around like I don't know how to get ready, and Brett runs his fingers through his hair. "You take the bathroom first."

He tries to open the door, but it's locked. He knocks. "Val? You in there?"

"Just a minute," Val calls. Brett steps back from the door, waving his hand in front of his nose. "It may be more than a minute." He steps out into the hallway and comes back in shaking his head. "A couple of Val's caddy friends are out there."

"Can you change in Val's room?" I ask.

He gives me a look. "Someone's in there."

I grin at him. "You people throw some serious parties."

Brett shrugs, giving me a proud smirk.

"Here," I say, glancing around. "Let's just both change in here. We've gotta hurry."

"All right," he says, pulling open a drawer as I scooch out of his way.

I grab the one-piece bathing suit Lauren issued me at check-in on Friday and the pair of resort-logo shorts. I check to make sure he's not looking at me. Like he's got eyes in the back of his head, he says, "I'm not looking."

"I know," I say and turn around, pulling my shorts off. I wrestle the bathing suit up my legs and then turn toward him just in time for a full view of that spectacular ass of his. It strikes me that I've seen him naked twice now but have yet to even kiss him. We're definitely working out of order here.

As he pulls a pair of boxer briefs up over it, I let out a sort of gasp-snort-laugh thing, which gets his attention. He grins at me. "Are you looking at me?"

"No!" I shout, with a massive grin of my own. "I was just making sure you weren't looking at me."

"I said I wasn't gonna look."

"I didn't know if I believed you."

"I slept in this bed with you last night without laying a finger on you. Does that not count for something?"

"Just hush so I can get dressed," I say, turning toward the wall and pulling my shirt off and the bathing suit up. When I turn around, he's sitting on the bed, putting on socks. "Thank you, for not looking," I say, tugging up my shorts.

"How do you know I didn't?" he asks and then flashes

me that smile that makes me want to spend the day in this bed with him.

"I'm done!" shouts Val from the bathroom.

Brett stands. "I'm going in," he says like a soldier getting ready to do battle. "Damn," he says as he shuts the door behind him, letting some of the stench into this room. I feel his pain.

BRETT PULLS his truck up to the gate of the lagoon pool. "Do you have the code for the gate?"

"Oh, crap. Somewhere." I pull out my phone.

"It's 8763," he says.

I let my shoulders sag. "Thank you."

He shrugs like it was nothing.

"No, I mean for letting me stay with you and for dinner and for fun and for listening and for helping me feel like myself for the first time in a really long time."

He shakes his head like he doesn't know what to say, color pouring into his cheeks.

"Sorry," I say, my own cheeks heating. "Ugh. Okay. Bye," I say, and then in some sort of effort to maximize this moment or maybe to sabotage myself, I reach over to kiss him on the cheek. But at the last second, I decide to make it his lips, and he sort of turns weird, too, and I find myself kissing his nostrils.

"God," I say under my breath as I pull away and get out of the car as quickly as I can.

THE LAGOON POOL during the light of day at work is quite the different scenario than it was Saturday night with Brett. Everyone was spot on about the parents. They are in hog heaven in this place. And they drink...boy, do they drink. I have worked a few of the stations now, and one of them is the tiki bar, where I made more mango daiquiris in an hour than I ever knew could be consumed.

I tried to put my housing situation out of my mind this past weekend, but today, the idea looms that there may not be a place for me to live. I can't do anything about it at the moment, so I spend my time thinking about my mis-kiss this morning. My stomach churns at my idiocy.

One thing about this job is that I don't have my phone on me. My shorts have no pockets, and I learned that's for a reason. They want us focused on serving guests, not on our phones. It's fine...it's just going to take some detoxing.

I retrieve my purse from my dedicated locker and see that I've got a few texts. One is from Samantha, wishing me a great first day. Another is from a friend I used to do yoga with checking in for the first time in probably six months, wanting to know if I'll meet her at a class tomorrow. She's probably the only friend I have who's not up to speed on my life. A third is from my mom in California, asking if I've come to my senses yet. Insert eye roll. And a fourth is from Brett.

Did you survive? If so, come meet some of us at Dolphin's Fin around six. Half-price pitchers.

Relief floods my soul. I didn't screw everything up with my weird kiss. At least it would appear that way.

Knowing my housing dilemma, my supervisor lets me cut out early. I walk to Housing and find a heavy-set, middle-aged lady sitting at a front desk, typing on her keyboard, not giving me a second thought.

"Hi," I say.

She turns slowly and meets my eyes with a hint of unwarranted incredulity. "Yes?"

"I'm Kylie McBride. I started work here today. On Friday afternoon, Lauren gave me this key card for 1624, but it's occupied."

She takes the card and sets it down on the counter then keys something into the computer. "Yes, that one's taken." She turns back to me with raised eyebrows and her lips tight in a thin line.

I'm teetering on being put out, but I'm trying to keep a positive attitude. "Can I get the card to the one Lauren intended to put me in? I'm sure she just keyed the wrong number in."

Another girl in her mid-twenties plops down in the chair beside this woman and takes a sip of a cup of steaming-hot something. She winces and scrunches up her face.

"Too hot?" I ask, hoping to open a friendly dialogue.

"God yes. I think I burned my tongue."

"I'm Kylie McBride. I started here today." I point to the lady next to her. "I was just telling her that Lauren gave me the wrong key card on Friday."

The girl rolls her eyes. "I hate to say this, but I'm so glad she's gone. She made a mess of our system. She wouldn't listen to me. Every time I'd try to train her on something, she'd just hold her hand up and say, *I got it,* so finally I was like *fine.* If you got it, then go ahead and mess everything up and see if I care. It's not my butt on the line."

I dig deep to exercise patience. "Right. So I was wondering if I could get the key card to the correct housing unit."

She sits up straight, poised in front of her computer, all business. "Name?"

"Kylie McBride," I say, not mentioning I just said it a second ago when I introduced myself to her.

The girl types. "One y?"

I think about that a minute, not sure where she thinks the y should go. "Yes, in Kylie."

She types quickly and then hits the return button with finality. Then she repeats the pattern. The furrow of her brow does not set my mind to ease.

"This is weird," she says, then types more...lots more. After a few moments of this, she meets my gaze, her expression taking on a contrite manner that I really wish it did not. "So, I've got some bad news."

No, not that. Anything but that.

"The housing that Lauren placed you in was occupied as of last Sunday."

I smile through gritted teeth. "Yes, I do realize that. I'm here now to get the key to the correct housing."

"We've got quite a waiting list for housing."

"Yes, I was told that during the interview process, but I got the email last Friday that said my housing had been accepted."

"Oh, yeah, that went out by mistake to all employees. We sent a second email retracting it."

My patience is wearing about as thin as a thread. "I did not receive a second email. Had I received a second email, I would have made alternate plans." I leave out the fact that, had this housing not gone through, I would never have been able to come here. I would have kept my plans quiet until I figured something else out.

She squints at me, pointing at my phone. "You should check your spam folder. Did you set us up in your address book as we strongly suggested in our original communications?"

I exhale a deep breath. "No, because I was receiving those emails just fine." I go to my email on my phone and look in the spam folder, and there sits an email from Destiny Dunes with the subject line RETRACTION. My heart sinks all the way to the ground, and I could collapse right here in this business office.

I close my eyes and then open them slowly. "So there are no openings in any other housing units?"

"No. Sorry," she says, looking not sorry. "But you are on the waiting list."

I stare at her for a minute longer, and when she starts typing into her computer again, clearly not on my case, I finally turn and walk out.

I SPEND hours on the couch at the business center, scouring websites for a place to stay, but it's hopeless. Everywhere I've called or checked out needs first and last month's rent, and I just don't have it—not even close. I can't bring myself to ask Samantha for more money. She's already done so much for me. And I'm damn sure not going to ask Joshua.

The problem is I've got to have somewhere for the night. I can't just keep staying here with Brett. He's only offered me a place to stay through the weekend, and time's up.

Something's gotta give. I simply don't have money and I don't have a credit card, or any credit, actually. I want to pull my hair out for fluffing through life up until now, relying on someone else to support me. As much as I hate to admit it, I've been a carbon copy of my mother. I thought I was so different from her because I wasn't going to let myself be humiliated by a cheating husband. But I see now that I can't do this on my own. I need help.

I consider calling my mom and cringe. I don't know which is worse, calling her or him. She's already told me I should go back to Joshua and forgive him. But my mom's self-esteem doesn't even chart. She thinks no woman can do anything without a man. I can't stand to prove her right.

I pull up my dad's contact on my phone, pacing as I stare at it for a long time before finally hitting his number. He answers. "Hello, sweetie, how are you?"

"I'm good," I lie.

"Still down South or have you made your way back home yet?"

"I'm still here."

"Well, that's unfortunate."

I collapse onto the couch. "Dad, he cheated on me. Do you understand that?"

"What I understand is that I paid a hundred grand for a wedding that didn't happen. You running off like this is an embarrassment to our family. It's an embarrassment to our company, and it's an embarrassment to me. You're lucky I don't sue you for the cost of this wedding."

My stomach climbs up into my throat. I can't believe he's saying this stuff to me. I've always known he was ruthless in business, but I never knew he would be that way with me.

"I assume you're calling because you need money?" he asks.

I wipe a tear away. "No. I'm just checking in."

"Look, sweetie, I love you. But this is nonsense. You can't just leave your life and everything you know because your fiancé had a simple indiscretion. He's sorry about it. It happens. Joshua is a good man and he will take care of you for the rest of your life. I'm not always going to be here to do it, you know?"

I clench my eyes shut, digging deep inside for fight, but I don't know if I have any left.

"If you're ready to come home, just say so. I'll send you enough to get back here. I'll reserve you a room halfway for tomorrow night. I don't want you to drive tonight."

"I need to go," I say.

"That's a standing offer," he says like he's giving me the moon. I click the phone off and drop my face into my hands.

13

BRETT

I order our last pitcher of beer from the bar and peer at the door while I wait. I don't mean to be checking it every fifteen seconds, but I can't help it. I want to see Kylie.

Last night, listening to her tell about the life she just left made me more interested in her. She's everything I've worked to avoid since I got caught up in Madison two years ago, but somehow, she's got me intrigued. She's either really brave for stepping away from the life she had without a net or really naïve.

Her weird kiss this morning has kept me smiling all day. It seemed like the first time she'd ever gone in for a kiss. She's made me feel like a middle schooler with a crush all day.

I take the pitcher of beer to the standing table Tori has for us.

"It's seven thirty. She's not coming," Tori says, taking a cup.

I fake confusion, but I'm sure I'm caught. "What are you talking about?"

Tori rolls her eyes and holds her cup out.

I pour her a beer and concede. "I wasn't looking for her. I thought Logan and Cohen might be coming. Logan worked the lunch shift, so he should be off. Just wanted to see if I needed to get one or two pitchers."

She studies me. "Liar."

"What?"

"You slept with her last night, didn't you?"

"No. I mean, yeah, we slept, but we didn't hook up."

She shakes her head at me, staring me down. I freaking hate it when she does that.

I stand up straight and face her. "What?"

"You were all over her last night."

"So? You and Val were messing around."

"Val's gay."

"He's been with women before," I say.

She just drops her head to the side.

"Who says I'm interested in Kylie?" I ask.

"That goofy smile you've had on your face all day."

I sigh, caught. "I'm not gonna let it get out of hand, okay?"

"You're going to be able to turn it off like you always do?"

"Of course."

"All right," she says, taking a sip of her beer, sounding wholly unconvinced.

We stand in stubborn silence for a while, until Jack Massey steps up to us. "You two are a lively duo."

"Fuck off," I say, not in the mood to spar.

"Damn. I know you hate me, but usually you're good for a little banter."

Tori glances away, the expression on her face revealing how much this asshole hurt her. I'd give anything if she could shake him, but I'm starting to think it's not possible.

It's been at least eight or nine months since they were together. My blood boils thinking about what he did to her. "You know, you don't have to come say hi to us. You can pretend we don't exist all day long."

He looks between the two of us. "I don't want to be an asshole."

"Too late for that," I say.

He lets out an irritated breath. "I don't want to be an immature asshole. How's that? I'm trying to be civil."

"Well, try fucking off next time," I say, knowing I'm taking my frustrations out on him. He's an easy target.

"It's fine," Tori says. "Just...whatever." She takes a drink of her beer.

I'm about to stand up and say something else to Jack when he turns his head with a surprised smile and says, "Hey."

Kylie walks up to us zombie-like, the color drained from her face.

"What's going on?" I ask.

"I um..." She looks around like she's trying to place herself and can't. "I think I might have to go home."

"You sick?" Tori asked.

"No, not Brett's house. My dad's house in Oklahoma."

A stab of pain shoots through my heart. "Why?"

"Turns out I never had housing here to begin with. I got an automated email that said I did, but that was some kind of systems glitch, and they sent a retraction, but that went to my spam."

"I know this town's expensive, but you can find something around here," Jack says.

Kylie rubs her forehead. "I called a few places that I found online. Funny thing, they want money now."

"Your dad can't loan you a couple hundred bucks?" Tori asks.

Kylie closes her eyes, looking sick.

"It's complicated," I say, hoping to keep her from having to explain her situation.

"I called him," she says, and I wince, knowing how difficult that must have been, and fearing what that means for her... and for me, selfishly. I don't want her to leave, and I damn sure don't want her back with an asshole who cheats on her. "He said he'd pay for one hotel room on my drive back home."

As the disappointment falls onto my shoulders, Tori cuts me a look.

"You're going back to Oklahoma?" Jack asks.

She shrugs. "I don't know what choice I have."

Tori's stare paralyzes me. She's just being protective of me, but it still puts me in the awkward position of not being able to offer Kylie my place to stay any longer.

"This is bullshit," Jack says, tapping into his phone then holding it up to his ear. "Julia. Hey. Is employee housing at capacity?" He pauses. "Can we squeeze an extra employee in somewhere? She'd be fine with a small space." He looks at Kylie for confirmation, and she nods quickly. "Can you look again in the morning? I know, just humor me, okay? Thanks. Sorry for calling during off-hours."

The look of hope on Kylie's face crushes my heart. I hate that Jack made that call, trying to be the savior when he knows he can't do anything about this.

He sighs and looks at her. "It's not looking good. She was pretty sure. And even if she found something, she'd be obligated to give it to the next person on the list."

Kylie's shoulders sag, and she nods.

We all stand in silence, Tori pointing her glare at me,

making sure I stay on track, and it takes all that's in me to keep quiet.

Jack tosses up his hands. "Fuck it. Stay with me."

The serious look on Jack's face makes my stomach roll over like that one time I tried sushi. Kylie looks up at him, seeming like she might consider it.

"I have a two-bedroom. Stay with me till you get on your feet. I'd be happy to have you." Jack smiles at her like a clueless idiot.

Tori's eyes go wide, and then she collects herself, watching Kylie for a response.

"No, I couldn't," Kylie says, but she looks very much like she could.

"I'm serious," Jack says. "Why not? The two of them can vouch I'm not an axe murderer."

"I'm not vouching for jack shit," I say.

He purses his lips at me. "Come on, man. I know I'm not your favorite person, but you know me. Tell her. She needs somewhere to stay and I don't hear you offering."

I'm about to wear the enamel off my teeth when Tori says, "She can stay with me." We all turn to her with shocked expressions, none more surprised than my own. Tori frowns at all three of us. "What? It's fine. She can."

"What about Janelle?" Kylie asks.

"Now that she's with Chris, she's never there. If he wasn't in the picture, it'd be a different story, but for now, it's okay. I can't offer you her room, but I can let you sleep on the couch."

"I can offer her a room," Jack says, because he can't ever leave well enough alone.

Kylie looks between the two of them, considering.

"It's fine," Tori says. "I promise. And I'm definitely not an axe murderer." She even tosses in the rarest of smiles. So now she's not only asking, she's begging. She's as jealous of the possibility of Kylie and Jack as I am.

Kylie shakes her head, mouth open in incredulity. "I can't thank you enough for this. I promise I'll pay you back rent when I get paid and on my feet."

Tori waves her off. "It doesn't cost me anything. The resort takes Janelle's half whether she's there or not."

Kylie beams at her. "Thank you." She lets out a deep breath, her shoulders popping up, then dropping, a smile stretching across her face.

"Have a beer," Jack says, pointing at my pitcher, and I could strangle him with my bare hands. Not that I don't want Kylie to have any, but I just don't want him to take all the credit for every damned thing around here.

"Okay," she says with a grin. "I'm just gonna run to the restroom." She darts off, and Jack shrugs at us. "Neither of you were offering."

He walks away, and I turn to Tori, who is pretending to be casually moving to the music and checking out the scene. "You want to explain yourself?" I ask.

She meets my gaze. "No," she says, challenging me with her no-bullshit eyes. I challenge right back. We've been at this with each other forever. She rolls her eyes. "Just leave me alone about this, okay?"

"Like you've been leaving me alone about Kylie?"

"There's no threat of me falling for her."

"You think that's what I'm gonna do?" I chuckle, picking up my beer. "You're high."

"Keep telling yourself that if you need to."

I consider her. "Are you ever gonna let him go?" She glares back at me, but the hurt in her eyes says there's more to that story.

Kylie arrives back at the table and sets her bag on a stool.

I'm not sure what to say. I've just completely screwed her over by not offering for her to stay at my place. But she doesn't seem bothered by that at all. She points to the pitcher. "May I?"

I nod, and she walks to the bar and grabs a plastic cup from a stack. Tori just rolls her eyes at me and leaves.

Kylie comes back over and picks up the pitcher. "I swear, I thought I was done. I can't believe I called my father. God, I know better." She takes a drink of the beer and stares at the cup like she's never had it before. She downs the rest and sets it down. "Man, I feel good right now."

I pour her another beer.

"No," she says, holding both hands up. "I'm not drinking your alcohol again."

"It wasn't my alcohol that you drank last night."

"Still. I'm not going to get in anyone's way these next few weeks. I'm just going to keep to myself and utilize that business center as much as possible, trying to find a way to bring in some more money quickly. Let me tell you, the last couple of hours have been an eye opener. Everyone wants first and last month's rent, plus deposit, fees, and all kinds of stuff. I don't know what I was thinking coming down here." She takes another long drink of the beer I poured her. "Now that I see what it's going to really cost to live, I've got to step up my game."

Cohen comes up to the table and pats me on the shoulder. "Wild party last night, man."

"Yeah, but it wasn't on purpose."

"Those are the best kind." He points at Kylie, squinting one eye. "Kylie, right?"

"Yep. And you're...Logan?"

"Cohen. Logan's my cousin."

"Yes, I knew that. Sorry."

"No problem. You've got a lot of names to keep up with. Brett told me at lunch the other day that they stuck you with him and Val for the weekend. Are you the one who cleaned their house?"

"Yeah, as a thank you for letting me stay for the weekend."

"That place was rank. How'd you get the stench out?"

"You're one to talk," I say. "Your place is just as bad as ours was."

"Yeah, I've got to get Logan off his ass to help me clean our place. Our moms are coming this weekend."

Kylie's eyes go wide. "I'll do it...for forty bucks...if you can provide the cleaning supplies?" She turns to me. "Or if I can borrow yours?"

I shrug.

Cohen studies her. "Seriously?"

"I'm totally serious. But you'll have to pay me in cash that day."

He squints as he considers the offer.

"You think a girl is gonna want to sleep with you in that filth?" I add. Not that I want Kylie in Cohen and Logan's unit or anyone else's, for that matter, but if this gets her on her feet sooner, hell yeah, I'm in her corner.

He meets Kylie's hopeful gaze. "Done."

She grins. "Can I do it tomorrow after work? I can come straight there."

"That works for me." He turns to me. "We'll come to your house while she's at ours."

She clasps her hands in front of her chest. "Awesome."

He hits me on the shoulder. "I like this girl, Brett. You could do much worse."

This is where I should explain that it's not like that, but I really don't mind him thinking we're together, especially since Kylie's getting ready to be up close and personal in his house.

Simone and Bailey come up to our table, and she hugs both of them and tells them about her day. I realize the more people who discover her, the more relationships she's going to build. She's going to meet guys and they'll like her. They'll want to date her, and they're definitely gonna want to hook up with her. If I don't make my move soon, someone else will.

14

KYLIE

Tori's unit is laid out exactly like Brett's. Same art on the walls, same vinyl couch, same tile flooring. But the vibe in this place is definitely more cold and stony. Maybe it's because Tori's not a morning person. I passed her in the hallway this morning on my way to the bathroom, and she didn't even look at me, much less say good morning. I get the distinct feeling she's regretful she asked me to stay with her.

I was so thankful when she offered, because I've only spent a little bit of time with Jack. While he seems perfectly harmless, he may not be. Tori and Brett don't like him, even though they appear to be some form of frenemies with him. But he gives the impression that he's a nice, helpful guy. Part of me wishes I would've taken him up on his offer to stay at his place. But the other part, ridiculously, wants to stay as close to Brett's unit as possible.

It's stupid. I know. Because Brett clearly isn't interested in me and maybe even has some doubts about me. Of Jack, Tori, and him, Brett was the only one who didn't offer me a place to stay. His silence spoke volumes that he wanted me out of his house. I try not to read too much into it, because he was so kind to let me stay for the weekend. But I thought we were getting closer.

I walk to Cohen and Logan's unit, which is right next door to Brett's. Cohen answers and greets me with a smile. He's maybe a couple of inches taller than me with rich, dark hair shorter than Brett's but not too short. His distinctly blue eyes contrast with his hair color, and his nose sits crooked, which only makes him cuter than your typical hunk with a perfectly chiseled nose.

"Hey. Come on in," he says with a deep tone to his voice.

Upon first glance, I assess that the job might be slightly less taxing than the one on Saturday, but not by too much. The place is, of course, exactly like Tori's and Brett's—the same décor, the same teal faux leather couch and recliner, and at least one picture of sand dunes like in Tori's unit.

I don't see any food lying in pans on the floor, but the dishes in the kitchen spill out of the sink onto the counter-tops, and there's some sort of slop on the kitchen floor that was never cleaned up.

"I'm guessing you don't use your kitchen?" I ask.

"Not since it got like that. I've been staying at my girl-friend's place for a few months, but we just split."

"I'm sorry."

"Are you still okay with doing this now that you've seen what you're up against?" he asks.

I glance around. "Absolutely. You said you had cleaning supplies?"

"Yeah, they're around. Check under the sinks." He pats two twenties sitting on a shelf by the door. "Here's your money. Are you sure this is enough? Forty?"

I want to ask for more, but the idea of two twenty-dollar

bills sitting there for me to grab like a thief after I finish here is like an oasis in the desert. "Yes, it's fine. Thank you."

"Would it be weird if I asked you to do my laundry? I'd throw in an extra ten."

"Not weird at all." I don't mention I was planning to do it as part of the forty. This job couldn't possibly be going any better. "Is any of this stuff yours?" I look around at random socks and boxer shorts lying on the floor.

"All mine is in my room. Shit, you don't want to touch Logan's underwear." He goes for a pair nearby.

"No, seriously. Leave it. I got it." I pray there's a pair of rubber gloves under that sink.

He scans me from top to bottom and shrugs. "All right then. I guess I'll leave you to it."

I walk him to the door. It feels weird, staying in this stranger's house while he leaves, seeing him out.

He points to Brett's unit. "I'll be next door if you need me. Do you want my number?"

"Sure." I hand him my phone and he types it in. He hands it back and I text, *Hello from Kylie.*

He looks down at his phone and then up at me. "Cool." He waves, his smile getting somehow cuter as it extends across his face.

When he leaves, I chew on my lip like I've done something scandalous. As weird as it sounds, my cleaning this house for money feels like a screw you to my dad and to Joshua, and especially to my mom, who would sooner slit her own throat than be someone's maid. But I feel good about this...really good. It may be the giddiness of knowing I'm doing something on my own without my father's money, but I've never been more excited to roll up my sleeves.

15

BRETT

I sit at my dining room table, finishing my spaghetti dinner from a box, listening to Logan and Val play some stupid video game. I never got into them because we couldn't afford them in my house growing up. It was more about work and survival. I brought one home for Matthew when I started working here years ago, so he's barely known a life without them. But for me at sixteen with a job and school, the moment had passed.

A knock sounds at the door, and I open it to find Cohen on my doorstep. "Come on in," I say, eyeing him. I know from Logan that Cohen was waiting for Kylie to get to their place so he could let her in to clean it. The idea of Kylie being alone in a house with a guy like Cohen makes me itchy. Cohen's not only a good-looking guy, he's a decent guy...someone I've found easy to talk to around here.

"What's up, man?" Cohen asks, walking inside.

"Not much," I say. "Did Kylie make it?"

"Yep. She's there now."

"Cool," I say, waiting for him to expound, but he doesn't. He walks over and plants himself in front of the television, arms crossed over his chest. "You want a beer?" I ask Cohen as I head toward the kitchen.

"Are you having one?" he asks.

"Nah. I could use a break."

He follows me. "Yeah, me, too. How are things coming along with Kylie?"

I toss my microwavable paper dish into the trash and put my fork in the dishwasher, taking a minute to think about this. When I meet Cohen's gaze, he's got his eyebrows up, waiting.

I shrug. "Nothing's coming along. We're just hanging out."

"You're not interested?" Cohen asks, relentless.

"Why the fuck do you care?"

He holds up both hands with a smile on his face. "Never mind."

He starts to walk out of the kitchen, but I nudge him. "Wait. Sorry. It's just..." I check the living room, where Val and Logan are caught up in their game. "I don't know. I'm figuring that out."

"You're figuring out if you're interested in her? It's usually not that difficult. Either you think she's hot or you don't."

"She's hot. I don't think that's arguable," I say, and he shrugs with a nod of agreement. "It's just that I don't want anything serious."

"Then tell her that up-front."

"She's not that kind of girl."

"You think she's the serious type?"

"She just got out of a relationship. She was engaged, actually."

"Then she may be good with a hookup. Something to get her mind off the other guy."

I wince, not wanting to be a rebound guy. "I don't know. I don't think she's really like that. I may not be a hundred percent comfortable with it even if she was." I shake my head at myself. "I don't fucking know." I get two beers out of the refrigerator after all and hand him one.

Cohen takes the beer and rests against the counter. "It's not rocket science, man. Have you thought about asking her out on a date? You're allowed to date a girl without it being a relationship."

Heat seeps up to my chest and to my neck. "It's been a while since I've taken a girl on a date."

He blinks at me. "How long has it been?"

I stare down at the beer in my hand that I don't even want, thinking about my fucked-up childhood and how I spent my high school and college years working crazy hours and trying to take care of my brother while my mom was getting sober and trying to go to school. And then I think of Madison, and how we went from hooking up to a full-blown relationship in zero to sixty. There were no dates, just a relationship that went sour when she found she couldn't be my top priority. "My life just hasn't really shaken out that way. I've been more of a hookup kind of guy."

Cohen nods as if this makes sense, but he's frowning.

"Why, do you date?" I ask him.

"Well, yeah. I mean, I do hookups, too, but I take girls on dates, for sure."

I scratch the stubble on my chin. "How does that usually go?"

"You mean like...where do we go, or..."

I feel like a tool asking this. "No, I can probably figure that part out. I mean, if you know it's not gonna be a quick hookup, then do you just keep going on the dates till you know it's right or... Screw it. Just forget it. I don't know what the fuck I'm saying." There's no sense in me asking these questions. I can't get anything started with her, anyway. I try to walk away, but he pulls me back in.

"Look, man. Keep getting to know her. You don't have to figure this out right away. Just keep hanging with her for now."

I frown at him. "If you weren't my friend, you'd be asking her out right now, wouldn't you?"

He looks guilty.

I point my beer can at him. "And fucking Jack Massey's already sniffing around."

He lifts his eyebrows in concession. "I see your point. Look, I know you've got some personal shit going on that's holding you back. But maybe this girl's worth putting yourself out there for."

I think of all the times I have lain in bed and dreamed of being a normal guy who has a real relationship with a woman...gets married and buys a house in the suburbs somewhere with a German shepherd running around like in the movies. Then I remember what happened last time I tried to have a relationship.

I shake my head. "I can't do a relationship. I've got to focus on my family."

"I get it. I know you're putting your brother through school, and you've got your mom and your grandma to take care of. But it doesn't mean you can't like a girl or at least kiss her."

The idea of this both gets my blood pressure going and scares the shit out of me. "Really?"

"Yeah. Otherwise you're sailing right into the friend zone, and there's no coming back from that. Kiss her, and that lets her know you're interested. She still might go out with Jack Massey or some other guy who sees a new girl around here to pounce on, but at least she'll know you're a contender."

A kiss. That's not dangerous. And it's not a relationship.

I chuckle, looking down at my beer. I set it down. "Thank you."

He shrugs. "I didn't do anything."

I head toward the front door, and he follows me. "Where are you going?"

"To your house."

16

KYLIE

I'm bringing a plate in from the living room when a knock sounds at the door, and I freeze, not sure what I'm supposed to do. I creep toward it on tiptoes and glance through the peephole. It's Brett. I breathe a sigh of relief, and my stomach starts spinning like it does when I see him.

"Hey," I say, wishing these guys had a mirror that I could have checked myself in before answering the door.

"How's it going?"

"About the same as Saturday."

"I wanted to see if you could use some help."

"Thanks, that's really sweet, but I've got this."

He scratches his chin. "Listen, can I talk to you a minute?"

"Yeah," I say, and we walk over to the couch and sit.

"I feel really weird about last night," he says.

I almost ask him if he means Monday morning, because I feel weirder about that oddball kiss than anything, but I just wait for him to go on.

"I should have offered you to stay longer with me if you

needed to. I just wasn't expecting your housing not to come through, and—"

"Please," I say, cutting him off, "don't think another thing about it. I never would have expected you to have me at your place for longer than the weekend, and I didn't even expect that. It's fine. I appreciate everything you've done—"

His lips are on mine before I can comprehend what's happening. His fingertips brush the nape of my neck, and then they thread through my hair. My body's reaction finally catches up with what's happening, my chest lighting up like a million hummingbirds are flying around a sanctuary. He pulls away and meets my gaze, his eyes lazy, his lip curling up in a little smile.

He clears his throat and stands up. "I'm gonna help." He walks into the kitchen, leaving me in a puddle on the couch. In a moment, he comes out with a trash can and picks up a bottle, tossing it in. In another life, I would tell him we should separate the plastic and aluminum for recycling, but I'm not sure my voice works at the moment. So instead, I get up and walk into the kitchen, begging the smile on my face to stop being so obnoxious.

I get a load going in the dishwasher and hand-wash the rest of the dishes. Brett squeezes by me with the trash can, and I still, wondering if he will touch me or try to kiss me again, but he just sets it down and then points to the kitchen sink cabinets, which I'm blocking. "May I?"

"Sure," I say, shutting the dishwasher door and scooting aside. He peruses the cleaning stuff, picking up a few bottles, and then squeezes back by. I find that the desire inside me has amped up like a race-car engine, but I tell my body to chill.

Brett disappears into the back of the unit while I work in the kitchen. A while later, from the hallway, the washer buzzes and I head over to the stackable units to transfer the laundry to the dryer.

Brett comes out into the hallway. "I'm done with the bathroom."

"Thanks," I say, tossing underwear into the dryer.

"You're doing their laundry?" he asks.

"Just Cohen's. He's paying me an extra ten bucks. He seems like a nice guy."

"He is."

I start the dryer and then turn around, resting on it. He holds back a grin, and I do the same. I jerk a thumb toward the living room. "I'm just gonna go get the broom."

"I'll wipe down the tables and stuff in the living room," he says, but neither of us moves.

I chew on my lip, looking down at my shriveled hands. "You're really sweet to help me with this."

"I have an ulterior motive," he says, sliding his hands onto my hips. We're face-to-face, but neither of us makes a move.

"At least you're up-front about that."

"Mmm-hmm," he says, inching closer.

I can't figure out what to do with my hands, so I finally rest them on his shoulders. It's so weird. I can't remember feeling these kinds of butterflies with Joshua or anyone else before him.

He leans in and kisses me again, but this time he doesn't stop. We kiss, sweet and innocent at first, but it doesn't take long for us to get exploratory. We fall into a heavenly bliss of mouths and my hands on his chest and his hands on my waist and my back. He presses against me, our body parts grazing one another's, then he pulls away to kiss my neck, and then I kiss his scratchy jawline.

A shout from outside rocks me back to reality, and I pull

away from him, my lips swollen and my body panting. "I'm gonna put in this other load of clothes."

"Okay," he says, his eyes dreamy as he steps back from me and heads into the other room.

As I put another guy's pants into the washer, it dawns on me that what Brett needed in order to start something with me was separation. Whatever this is between us is brand spanking new. How could that work if we were in the same house? But now, he has the freedom to try something with me knowing we have our own space to exit to.

I sweep the floors while Brett wipes down everything and then follows after my sweeping with a mop. I'm so impressed by the fact that he's completely fine with cleaning another guy's house just so he can be with me. It's pretty dang sweet.

We finish the floors and put up the broom and mop in the kitchen closet, and he gets that kissing look again. I grin, trying not to look at him. "I saw two sets of clean sheets in the hall closet. Do you want to help me make up the beds?"

"Yep," he says and follows me down the hall.

We strip the beds and put on the clean sheets and comforters, then Brett tosses me onto Cohen's bed. I let out a girly giggle that I never knew I had in me. We get started again with a make-out session, but it's all very innocent. There are kisses full of grins, even some teeth knocking, plenty of teasing, and nothing that would devastate me if it was secretly recorded and blasted on socials.

The buzzer on the dryer sounds. "I need to go get that."

He pulls me back to him. "Cohen can do his own damn laundry."

"Not if I want his ten dollars." I peck him on the lips and roll off the bed and onto my feet.

I gather the laundry and then dump the load onto

Cohen's bed. As we start folding, Brett meets my gaze. "It's respectable, what you're doing here."

"Folding laundry?"

"Doing what you have to do to make it on your own and distance yourself from your old life. I imagine as a rich girl growing up on the slopes of Aspen, you probably didn't have to take too many cleaning jobs in order to get by."

"To be fair, I did have a very strenuous job at a high-end boutique when I was sixteen. How do you think I got to be such an excellent folder?" I display a T-shirt, draping it over my arm and motioning to it with my other hand.

Brett picks up a pair of Cohen's boxers, realizes what he has in his hands, and then tosses them at me. "I have my limits."

"Another man's underwear? That's your cleaning limit?"

"Yep."

I fold them and start a pile when my text alert sounds. I pull my phone out of my back pocket and see that it's Cohen.

How's it going?

I type back.

Good. Everything's done except your second load of laundry. It's in the dryer. Will probably be another hour just waiting on that.

Cool.

I re-pocket my phone, and Brett eyes me, folding a resort-issued polo.

"That was just Cohen checking in."

"Mmm," he grunts, and we fold in silence a moment. "He got your number?"

Do I detect a hint of jealousy? "Yep," I say, trying not to be weird.

He picks up a T-shirt and cuts his eyes at me. "Are you into him?"

I squint at him, holding back my grin. "Would you care if I was?"

He gives me a sly look without an answer, triggering a warmth to my center.

We finish folding and I find places for all the clothes in drawers. I turn around. "All done."

He holds his hand out to me, and I take it as we stand face-to-face, staring into each other's eyes, my whole body on alert down to my core.

"I'd care," he says.

My pulse is sent racing. I'm not sure what to infer from those two words, but I'm okay leaving it at that.

"Good to know," I say.

His mouth is on my neck and he's leaving soft kisses with bits of tongue. My eyes close and my head falls back instinctually. He pulls away and I meet his mouth with mine, my hands cupping his substantial shoulders. He's not buff like a bodybuilder or overly broad, but he's solid.

I am barely aware of a door shutting in the distance when Brett eases away from me, pinching my hip with a cute little grin. I straighten myself, checking my body for any evidence of my wanton lust for this man.

We walk out to find Cohen and Logan in the living room inspecting the place. There are two other guys with them who I don't recognize.

"Damn, girl," Logan says.

"Did you know our kitchen floors were white?" Cohen asks. "I always thought they were gray."

"Your second load of laundry is in the dryer," I say, "and the sheets are in the washer. I can come back and fold it all tomorrow if you're ready for me to get out of your hair tonight?"

Brett cuts his eyes at me, clearly not liking that option.

Cohen waves me off. "It's cool. Thanks, though."

"You did all this for forty bucks?" one of the strange guys asks, looking around. "This place was gross."

"Your place is even grosser," Logan says.

The one guy looks at the other guy. "We've got forty bucks."

"Yeah," the other one says. "My girlfriend won't come to my place until I clean it."

"It's fifty if you want me to do your laundry." I rethink that, not knowing how much laundry they have. "Actually, five per load. I put in the sheets before I leave. You can put those in the dryer and start them yourself. That's if you have a spare pair for me to replace the dirty ones with." I'm making all this up on the fly like this is my full-time business.

"Cool," one of the guys says. "Can you come tomorrow?"

I'm so tired I'm about to collapse, but my response is, "Absolutely."

I collect their info, and then Brett and I head out. I can't be sure, but it's possible Brett and Cohen exchange a look as they pass one another. I don't think I was supposed to see it, but I happened to turn around right as they met each other's gazes. I can't help wondering what that was about.

When we get outside, I'm curious if Brett will ask me to come to his place, but he walks with me in the direction of Tori's unit. This is definitely for the best. The kisses were luscious, but I don't think I'm ready for anything else tonight. If he'd have asked, it might have been hard to turn down.

When we get to the steps of Tori's unit, he stops and pockets his hands. Now he's going all shy on me?

"Thanks for helping tonight. I'd be there another hour if it weren't for you," I say.

"No problem."

I try to hand him a twenty, but he waves me off, so I put it away and adjust the strap of my purse. "I had fun, if that's possible while doing dishes."

"I had fun, too. I'm free tomorrow night," he says, eyebrows up.

I giggle. "No way. I'm doing tomorrow night's gig solo. But thanks for asking."

"Understood," he says and backs away. "Night, Kylie."

A massive letdown takes me over, because I was really hopeful for a final kiss for the night, but I've still got the ones from earlier to dream about as I drift off to sleep.

17

KYLIE

As I lean into the pool to grab a kickboard, a sharp pain shoots through my back and I stand up straight, pressing my hand on it like the boomers do on the arthritis management commercials. I think this is my body screaming for some yoga. I've abandoned my regimen since everything went to hell back home.

But the pain has come with its reward—a hundred and fifty beautiful dollars. Monday night's job led to Tuesday night's job, then one last night. While I'm so exhausted I have to make sure I don't pass out into the pool, I'm able to eat something other than peanut butter crackers for dinner tonight.

Brett checked in with me on Tuesday to say hi, but that's been pretty much it. He didn't respond to my response, which was left sort of open-ended, but I'm not freaking out. It's not like we slept together and things are weird or anything like that. We just kissed, he said he'd care if I was into another guy, and then we said good night. It's normal not to be talking every day...I think. Honestly, I have no idea.

I was in a years-long sham of a relationship. That's my whole level of expertise on the subject.

I don't have any more cleaning gigs lined up at the moment, so I've offered to take Tori and Brett out to dinner. It's not just an excuse to get to see him again. It kind of is, but I also do want to thank them both properly. We're going somewhere Tori says is excellent but cheap, which I'm extremely thankful for, because by the time I put some gas in my car and bought some food that had actual nutrition involved, I'm already down over sixty bucks.

"Hey," I hear and whip my head around to find Jack walking toward me in his suit pants and a shirt and tie. He looks a good ten years older than he has the other times I've seen him. But even so, he's seriously handsome—a bit devastatingly so, actually.

"Hey," I say with a smile. I glance him up and down. "Did you come for a swim?"

He gazes at the pool. "I wish. I actually came to see you. How's it going here at the pool?" he asks, glancing around like he's on Mars.

"It's good."

"Did you hurt your back?" he asks.

"Oh, no. That's just from overdoing it this week. I've been cleaning houses for some extra cash. I've had gigs three nights this week."

He looks at me like I've sprouted a unicorn horn. "You've been doing that on top of this job?"

"Yeah. It's just temporary, until I get on my feet."

"Do you want to leave all this behind and come to work in the business office with me?"

I shrug. "Sure. When do I start?"

"Monday. It's a temp job—two weeks. You'd be collecting data for an outreach initiative."

My heart rate quickens. "Wait, are you serious? This is a real thing?"

"Like I said, it's temp work. Nothing glamorous, but it pays a little more than you're making here."

I glance around, dumbfounded. "Can I do that—just leave my pool job for two weeks?"

"They'll redistribute staff. They do it all the time."

"What about after the two weeks?"

"You can come back here or we can see what else is available around the resort."

I grip the kickboard, the excitement shooting through my arms. "Really? It's that easy?"

He chuckles. "Yeah. Didn't they redistribute staff at your last company? I checked out your resume earlier. Hope you don't mind."

My chest constricts with guilt. I listed my dad's company on my resume and application and gave one of the HR women who I used to chat with as a reference. Her husband had cheated on her once and she was more than willing to help. I scratch my forehead. "Uh, sure."

"So you're in?"

I nod vigorously. "Yes. Absolutely."

"Come to the business office on Monday morning."

I shake my head. "I can't believe this." I open up my arms. "Thank you." I start to give him a hug, and then I pull away, quickly. "Wait, that's inappropriate...isn't it?"

He smiles. "I suppose it could be construed that way. Especially since you're in a bathing suit."

I give him a thumbs-up with a cluck of my tongue against my cheek. "Right." I punch him in the shoulder lightly. "Thanks a bunch."

He chuckles. "You're welcome. Hey, some of us are going

out for darts and pool tonight if you want to come. Bailey will be there."

"Thanks for asking, but I'm taking Brett and Tori out to dinner."

"Ah, well, I'd say bring them, but I doubt they'd want to be there if I'm there."

I narrow my gaze at him. "Someday, one of you is going to have to explain to me why you don't get along with them."

He steps back with a contrite smile on his face. "I'll see you Monday. Business Affairs."

I point at him. "Enter through the business center, right?"

"Yep."

I smile. "I'll be there."

As he walks away, my mind reels with possibility. This is my chance. It may only be a temp job, but if I show them I'm the best damn temp worker they've ever hired, maybe I can parlay this into an actual real job.

When I get home to Tori's unit, I find her on the couch painting her toenails. She's decked out in a skirt and top that's super cute on her, and her hair appears to have been pulled straight then curled. She almost always wears it in that bun on top of her head. It looks good that way—her signature style. But she's practically glamorous with it down.

"Wow. I better up my game," I say.

"Hey," she says, focused on her toes. "I'm bailing on the two of you tonight. Hope that's okay."

It would have been nice to have had her there, but it may be even nicer to have Brett to myself. "That's cool," I say. "What's up?"

She hesitates, then cuts her eyes at me. "I've got a date."

"Nice. Who with?"

She winces. "This...man."

"Okay," I say, taking a seat on the chair next to her.

"He's actually a dad of one of the kids who spent some time with us about a month ago. He and I talked a few times, and he was cool and all, but I didn't think anything about it."

"Clearly he did." That gets a hint of a smile from her and a blasé lift of her shoulder. But I can see she's impressed with herself. "Does he live here?" I ask.

"No, he's in town for business."

I try to imagine what business would bring someone to this town, because it's pretty much only a tourist town.

She glances up at me. "He's not married."

Is she a mind reader? "Okay," I say like I hadn't even thought about it, but I suppose my momentary silence spoke volumes. She inspects her toes, wiggling them. "Nice color," I say.

"Mmm."

I'm not sure I've seen her in this good of a mood since I've known her. "Do you mind if I grab a shower?"

"Knock yourself out. I'm leaving in just a bit. Y'all have fun."

"You, too."

I shower, shave, blow-dry, and curl, and then find some dressy shorts and a blouse that ties at my belly, exposing just a hint of skin on my waist. The last time I saw him, I was doing laundry and scrubbing floors, so I've got to remind him I'm a girl.

I lock up and head over to his unit, my stomach flipping as I knock on his door. Why am I nervous? He kissed me

Monday night, not the other way around. I just wish I would have heard a little more from him this week.

He opens the door and blinks. "Hey," he says, like he wasn't expecting me.

"Hey," I say, giving him a curious look. "Are you still up for dinner?"

"Yeah." He looks past me. "Where's Tori?"

Crap. I just assumed she told him. Now this is weird. Should I have canceled the whole thing? "She's got a date. She bailed on us."

"Who with?" he asks, more like a curious older brother than a jealous boyfriend, I think.

"A dad, actually, from about a month ago, she said."

"Really?" he asks.

I wince. "Maybe I wasn't supposed to say anything."

"It's fine." He looks around his living room like he's lost for a minute, and then he meets my gaze with a look like he's given up. "You ready?"

I can never leave well enough alone. "Is everything okay with you?"

"Yeah. Of course it is."

"Okay, because if this isn't a good time, we can totally reschedule for a night when Tori can come, too."

"No," he says and closes his eyes, shaking his head, and now I know something's up. He runs his hand through his hair and then steps back and looks me up and down. "I'm sorry. You look really good."

My belly goes giddy. "Don't be sorry about that." I peruse him in his button-down shirt with shorts, looking almost preppy, for him. It's so cute that he's made an effort. "You look good, yourself."

He takes my hand, and my nervous stomach trembles as

he rubs his thumb along my knuckle. "I'm just kind of new at this."

I'm super confused, because I know he's not new at dating girls. He had a slew of them on him the other night at the beach, and plenty were all over him on Sunday night at his house party, too. "What's *this*?"

He lets out a slow breath and then pulls me into his arms. "Just ignore me, okay?"

I make a face. "It's kind of hard to." I smile at him, but I'm still pretty confused and not at all confident of what's happening here. He pulls me toward the door. "Let's go. I've got an idea for tonight."

18

KYLIE

We drive about twenty minutes to a neighboring beach town, where Brett pulls into a parking lot in front of an outdoor marketplace. Vendors and food trucks with everything from oysters to ice cream line the place, with a live band in one corner and kids running through sprinklers in another. "This is pretty cool," I say as we walk into the fold, Brett taking my hand and smiling at me. It feels like we've stepped into another world.

"What do you like to eat? They've got pretty much everything," he says.

"What do you get when you come here?"

He points. "I like these soft pretzels."

"Brett, I'm getting you something better than a soft pretzel."

"All right," he says, and we keep walking. "But it's what I want," he mumbles under his breath, loud enough for me to hear.

I stop him. "Seriously? You want a soft pretzel?"

"They butter them and they're all doughy."

A woman behind the counter pulls a pan out of the oven

and places them in paper sleeves. Brett looks at me like a puppy dog wanting a treat, and it's too cute to resist.

"They do look pretty good," I say, walking over to the lady, and I order two. "What do you want to drink?" I ask him.

"Sweet tea," he says.

"Of course you do," I say. "You're a Southerner."

"You don't like sweet tea?" he asks.

I face the woman. "Can I do half and half?"

"Yes, ma'am," the lady says and pours our drinks. She hands us everything and we eat while we walk around.

"This is amazing," I say, holding up the pretzel.

"I told you," he says through a mouthful, trying not to smile.

We stand and watch the band while we finish the pretzels. He takes my paper and tosses it away with his, and then he pulls me toward a dock that's lined with boats. "Come on," he says. "I'll show you Robert's boat."

Robert's boat is the very last one of a strip of them. Brett steps onto it and then holds out his hand for me to take. I look around like we're being hunted by police. "Are we allowed to get on it?"

"Yeah. He's out of town."

"Still," I say.

"Would it make you feel better if I texted him and asked?"

I consider him.

"Seriously, he tells me all the time I can use the boat whenever I want."

"You've done this before?"

"A bunch of times."

I look him up and down. "With girls?"

He closes his eyes, caught. "Maybe once with a girl, but usually with Tori."

"She's not a girl?"

"Tori and other people. Cohen and Logan have been on here with me, too. Come on. Just get on."

I take his hand and step onto the deck of the boat. We walk around to the other side and peer out into the open water. "Wow. This is awesome," I say.

"Mmm-hmm," he says, gripping the railing. He pulls his keys out of his pocket and goes for the door to the cabin. "Want to go inside?"

"You have a key?"

"You really doubt me a lot, don't you?" Brett opens the door to the cabin, and we step into a tight living space with leather built-in sofas on either side, a small kitchen area with a booth for dining across from it, and a bed on the other side of the kitchen tucked compactly into the nose of the boat.

"Wow," I say. "This is super nice."

"Yep."

I point to the bed. "You and that girl you brought here that time..."

He holds up a hand. "I swear I have not had sex on this or any other boat, come to think of it."

I roll my eyes at him and walk the perimeter of the small area. "This is really cool."

He opens the refrigerator, which is full of drinks. "Want anything?"

I hold up my tea. "I'm okay with this, thanks," I say, feeling like Robert is going to step onto this boat any second and fire me.

He sits on the couch and props his feet up on the table. I

sit next to him, and he stretches and puts his arm on the couch behind me, holding back a grin.

"I see your game," I say.

"I don't have a game," he says, trying to appear innocent and failing miserably.

I smile at him, shaking my head. "I'm not gonna be the next in your line of a hundred and fifty-seven girls." I sound like I'm confident in this statement, but with how cute he's looking right now and how devastatingly attracted I am to him, I hope I can follow through with that statement.

"I'm serious," he says. "I didn't bring you here for that. I just think it's a cool place to come, and I know Robert's out of town this weekend and won't be here. It seemed like an opportunity. We can go?" he says, looking at me with a question on his face.

"We can stay, but only because I love boats, and that's one thing my family didn't do often growing up."

"Did your dad hate the lake, too?" he asks.

"Yeah, he's not really a fan of the water. What about you? Did you grow up on boats?"

"No, but Robert has taken me out on this one a few times."

"And he gave you a key to it?"

"Yeah. He has me come check on it from time to time. He'll have me fill the fridge with drinks, that kind of thing. I think it's his veiled way of making me try to relax. Sometimes I'll sit up top and just stare out at the ocean. It's a decent escape."

"Definitely," I say, nodding and looking around. I meet his gaze and he grins at me and then looks away. "What?"

"Nothing," he says, drumming his fingers on his cup.

I pull back from him. "Seriously, what?"

He drops his posture. "I just really want to kiss you, but

now I can't 'cause you'll think I brought you here to hook up."

I point at him. "See, I knew you brought me here for that."

He laughs. "I did not. I mean, if you wanted to, I wouldn't argue, but—"

I smash a throw pillow into his face and he snags it from me. "I'm just teasing. I don't even want to kiss you," he says. "Gross."

I feign shock. "Gross?"

"Yeah." He shudders. "Girls. Yuck."

I set my cup down in a holder and then pinch at his stomach.

"Quit it," he says, chuckling.

I hike a leg over his lap so I'm straddling him. "Gross? Really?"

He smooths a lock of my hair over my ear. "Completely."

I shake my head at him, and as I'm leaning in for a kiss, an alarm sounds in my brain, and I pull away and sit down beside him. "I meant to tell you I got a new job—a temporary one, but still."

He runs a hand through his hair, letting out a hard breath. "Yeah?"

"At the business office. Something about an outreach initiative."

"That's cool," he says, but his brow is furrowed. "How did that come about?"

This is the part I don't want to answer, but I need to. "Jack got the gig for me."

He turns toward me, his relaxed body language gone. "When did you see him?"

"He came to the pool earlier today."

Brett turns his head away from me, looking out at the ocean through a window.

"I know you're not a fan, but Jack's been really helpful to me. If he's a psycho or he's a terrible guy who's going to hurt me professionally, please let me know that and give me specifics. Otherwise, I could really use his help."

He inhales a sharp breath and then releases it, taking a drink of his tea. He swallows, looking down at the cup. "Just watch your back with him, okay?"

"So to be clear, he's not a serial killer?"

He rolls his eyes, shaking his head. "That doesn't mean he's not an asshole."

"An asshole, I can deal with. But for the record, he's been nothing but nice to me."

"Of course he has. You're hot."

I let my head drop to the side. As much as my girl parts do a happy dance at this statement coming from Brett, I'm not apt to buy it a hundred percent. I lift an eyebrow. "He's being nice. He's not even hit on me once."

"Just wait. It's coming."

"Is it so hard for you to believe that someone would just want to be helpful with no ulterior motive?"

He points at his own chest. "I thought I did help you."

"You did, and you've been fantastic. But why are you pissed at him for helping me the way he knows how?"

"Because he's trying to sleep with you."

"He is not."

"He is."

"I'm sure there are plenty of girls who'd be more than happy to sleep with him. There's nothing so special about me that he needs to go to these kinds of lengths."

I can see by the look on Brett's face that I've just screwed up epically. He turns away from me, shaking his head. "I knew it," he says under his breath.

"I don't know what you think you know, but I'm sure you're wrong."

"Go on," he says, motioning with his cup. "Go out with him. See what all the fuss is about."

I squeeze his leg, reminded of the fragility of the male ego, even for a guy as handsome and confident as Brett is. "I don't want to go out with him."

He looks at me like he's trying to gauge my honesty.

Because of what I've just gone through with Joshua, putting myself out there is tough. But Brett's vulnerability emboldens me. I may be making a stupid mistake, but there's something trustworthy about him that makes me want to take that leap. "In case I've been too subtle," I say, "I'm interested in you."

He gives me a skeptical look. "Yeah?"

I giggle. "Yeah. I'd even like you to kiss me right now."

He sets his cup down and then takes my hand. "What if I maybe brought you here with the intention of doing just that?"

"I'd say that sounds kind of fun."

He leans in and our lips meet. My core lights up as his hand rests on my hip, his thumb rubbing on the tiny spot of exposed skin on my stomach. It's unbelievable that one touch can wake me up so wholly from a nap I feel like I've been in for years. His hand grips my hip as our kiss becomes intense, and my body comes alive in that way that's so exciting but terrifying at the same time. I pull away to get ahold of myself.

He smiles at me, tucking a lock of hair behind my ear. "I haven't met anyone like you in a long time. Maybe ever."

I think of him on the beach that night, leaned into that

girl's ear, whispering something to her that was probably very close to what he just said to me. "How am I different?" I ask, because I really want to know what separates me from her and all the others.

"I don't know," he says, looking down at his hand, which is sliding around my thigh. "You're genuine. You seem to be your own authentic self at all times. Some girls aren't like that. They're on the chase. They're all about the catch and release. I feel like I'm in a game, not a relationship. Whoever blinks first gets their heart broken."

"I don't play that game," I say, my voice coming out quiet and serious.

He thinks for a moment, staring at the ground. "I'm not playing a game either, but I'm also not in a place to be in a relationship. I've got way too much going on in my personal life, and I can't bring another girl into it."

I frown. "Another girl?"

He shakes his head. "I don't have any other girls right now. But I did have one a while back. I got distracted from what was important...my family. When the newness wore off and I put my focus back on where I was needed, she couldn't hack it, and things ended badly. I can't lose focus again, not while we're trying to get through my grandmother's illness."

"What does your grandmother have?"

"Alzheimer's. She can't be left alone even for a half hour. One of us has to be with her all the time."

"I'm sorry," I say, rubbing his knee, taking all this in.

He clasps my hand. "I really like you, Kylie. I feel like I'm in purgatory here. I want to move things forward with you, but I can't do that right now."

"What can you do then?"

He considers this. "I can tell you that I'm not looking for

a quick hookup and then onto the next girl. I think about you when I wake up, when I'm walking to work, when I'm in between patients, when I'm going to lunch... You're pretty much on my mind every moment. I don't know if that makes me sound like a stalker or what. But it's true. I've never been like this before. It's freaking me out a little."

I giggle out of nervousness, I guess. I want to believe him, but my defense mechanisms are firmly in place thanks to the years of lies and hurt.

He takes my hand. "I don't know why I'm telling you this. I know I'm talking out of both sides of my mouth. I don't know what I'm trying to convince you of. I'm just saying how I feel, I guess."

I nod, meeting his gaze. "Mmm-hmm." I don't know what else to say or do other than to hear him out and see where he's going with this.

He stands up and paces. "Look. I'm not gonna lie. I've never thought I was a jealous guy. But I get jealous with you. I hate that Jack Massey's helping you find a better job and that he offered you to stay with him." He spits out the last part of his sentence. "I know guys are interested in you, and I know they're gonna be asking you out. It makes me nuts to think about you going out with them. But I also can't promise you anything with me. I know none of this is fair, and I'm not asking you for anything, I just..." He glances around the room like he's looking for answers.

My heart races through my chest, because I've never known this kind of passion from a guy. I stand up and walk to him. He meets my gaze, his eyes intense.

I run my hands over his shoulders. "I can't promise you anything either. But we can feel our way through this, if there is a *this* here?"

He stares at me. "I'm sorry I'm all over the place. I've

never been this way."

I smile at him. "I don't know what the heck I'm doing either."

He wraps his arms around me and brings me in for a hug, and we stand there like that, our hearts beating together for the longest time. We rock from side to side, almost like we're dancing, but there's no music playing except for the distant hum of the band.

The sound of footsteps on the dock outside, then a rattling on the door handle has us both looking that way.

"I think it's unlocked," comes a female voice I recognize, and I freeze as the door flies open and Bailey stands in the entryway.

"If there's someone in there, kick their ass, Bailey!" comes a guy's voice from behind her.

Brett's stance tightens and he folds his arms over his chest. "What the—" he starts, but he cuts his own words off as Jack Massey appears in the doorway.

"Holy shit," the guy I don't know says through a laugh. "It's Hargrove. How you doin', man?"

Brett blinks the guy into recognition, then his posture drops. "Hey," he says, holding his hand out to the guy, who ignores it and pulls Brett in for one of those guy hugs that approaches near-violent with hard slaps on the back.

"Fuck, what's it been, two years?" the guy asks, looking Brett up and down.

"At least that. What are you doing here?"

"Vacation." He backhands Brett on the chest. "I told Massey to call you but he gave me some bullshit story about thinking you were out of town for the weekend." The guy tosses up his hands. "Fuck, this is awesome. Let's have a beer." He seems to notice me for the first time. "Oh, shit. I'm sorry. We interrupted."

"No," Brett says, shaking his head, seeming to reorient himself. "This is Kylie. Kylie, this is Asher. He worked at the resort with us a few years back."

Asher takes my hand and sort of bows down to me, kissing it. "Hello, lovely Kylie." Damn. This guy's got game.

The girl I don't know smiles at Brett. "Hey, there."

The two of them hug, and then he pulls back from her, inspecting her. "You decided to keep him around?"

She slides her arm around Asher's waist. "He's hard to shake once he weasels his way in." She holds out her hand to me. "I'm Corinne. It's so good to meet you."

"Yes, same," I say, her smile catching on. These two seem like newlyweds. I glance down at her left hand and see a rock. Memories of my own engagement ring flood in, making me feel like a phony. These two clearly have the real thing.

I catch Bailey's gaze for the first time, and she's smiling, but it's not reaching her eyes. "Hey," she says, giving me a loose hug. She pulls away, staring at me like she's a mouse caught in a trap.

Jack meets Brett's hard gaze. "Sure we're not interrupting?" Jack asks, sounding sincere as he glances at me and then back to Brett.

"Nope," Brett says, holding Jack's gaze.

"Good. Let's get a beer," Jack says.

Asher puts one arm around Jack's shoulder and the other around Brett's. "The three dickheads, back in business," he says with a huge grin. "Who wants a shot of spiced rum?" he asks, and I'm taken aback when both Jack and Brett break out in reluctant smiles. I think this is some kind of inside joke between the three of them.

Jack glances at Brett. "He'll take two."

Brett considers Jack, looking like he wants to respond

but can't bring himself to do it. Instead he walks to the fridge. "We've got IPA, sour beer, and some of those seltzer drinks."

"Kylie," Bailey says, and I turn to face her. "Come outside with me. I want to show you this awesome boat across the way."

I follow her out the door, and she pulls me a few boats down and then faces me. "I just wanted to talk to you about why I'm here with Jack."

"Okay," I say with a shrug.

"I know that you're living with Tori now, and I don't want anything to be weird."

"What would be weird?"

"It's just that I'm not like *here* here with him. I mean...I'm not expecting anything. We work together and nothing can happen because of that. And, of course, because of Tori, too." She gives me a significant look.

I raise my eyebrows, waiting for the rest of her story.

She lets out a sigh. "I would appreciate it if you didn't mention that I came here with Jack."

"Okay, but aren't we all just having a drink together?"

"Yes, of course. That's all it is," she says as if she's convincing herself.

I take her hand. "Hey, it's fine."

Bailey scratches her forehead, scrunching up her face. "I just wish I didn't do this. I go for these unavailable guys who will never want me."

"Is Jack unavailable?"

"For all intents and purposes, yes. He's hung up on Tori. He's been hung up on her ever since they broke up."

"So, where does that put you?"

"It puts me in the same place I've been since the day I met him. The friend zone."

"Would you rather be in the friend zone or completely off the playing field?"

She frowns. "I do want to stay on the playing field."

"Then let's just go in and have a drink."

She smiles. "Cool." She starts to walk away, but I stop her. "Hey, so what's the story with Brett and Jack tonight? They seem to have put their differences on hold."

"Who knows with boys? But if I had to guess, I'd say neither of them wants to look like they're the immature one holding a grudge."

"Neither wants to air their dirty laundry?" I ask.

"Exactly."

I grin. "It's fun to watch them squirm around each other."

"I know, right? I can enjoy myself and settle in for the show now that you and I have talked. Thanks for being a good friend even though you don't know me."

"Thanks for trusting me."

She smiles, and we head back to the boat.

"Who is this girl, by the way?" I ask.

"Just met her tonight. She's with Asher."

"Ah, then this was a double date."

"No," Bailey says, hesitating outside the door to the cabin. "I was kind of in the right place at the right time, I think. I was in Jack's office talking when they came by to surprise him. Asher's the one who asked me to come tonight, not Jack."

For some reason, this makes me feel better about hiding the full details of the night from Tori. Not that she'll even care or ask me about it. Something tells me Brett won't want to rehash any of this with her either.

"However you got here, you're here," I say. "Let's go in and watch Brett and Jack act like they love each other."

19

BRETT

As much as I hate to admit it, I'm glad that Jack showed up. Things were getting out of hand with Kylie. I don't know why I can't seem to keep myself in check around her. She has this way of making me feel like things are going to be okay. There's something about her that's stabilizing in my world that's constantly upended. As much as I want to get close to her, I like her too much for that. I can't have a repeat of what happened with Madison.

"It's your turn, Hargrove," Jack says, looking me in the eye, daring me. Or fuck, maybe that's just how he looks at people.

"I'm no good at this game. I've done everything."

"I believe that," Bailey says, winking at Kylie.

"I bet there's plenty you haven't done," Jack says.

"If you're referring to trips to Monte Carlo, then yeah, I've never done that shit." I smile at Kylie. "I've never been to Aspen." Everyone drinks except for Kylie and Jack, and I'm sorry I said it.

Kylie smiles at him. "You ski?"

"I'm the king of the bunny slope," he says.

"Come on. I bet you're at least a six or a seven," she says.

He shrugs. "I can manage down a decent hill without breaking my neck. What about you?"

"I can ski past you down that same hill."

This gets a robust reaction from the group, and I sip my beer, looking away. The last thing I need right now is to see the two of them bonding.

Asher puts his arm around Corinne. "Corinne's a competitive ice skater."

She rolls her eyes. "When I was little. I'd bust my ass hard if I tried that now."

"Impressive," Kylie says. "So you can spin and jump and all that?"

"She can," Asher says. "She's being modest."

Corinne waves him off. "Never have I ever walked in on people having sex."

Bailey drinks, and everyone laughs. "My parents, when I was fourteen. Scarred for life."

"Anyone else?" Asher asks.

Kylie scratches an eyebrow, clearly uncomfortable.

"This is a stupid game," I say. "Who wants another drink?"

"I'll take one," Corinne says.

I look at Kylie and she nods.

Jack asks Bailey, "You want another one?"

"Okay," she says with that smile that conveys she really wishes we'd all leave her on the boat alone with Jack. That'd be fine with me.

I go over to the fridge, and Jack meets me there. "You had your chance to get rid of us," he says in a low voice.

I give him a look. "Like it was that easy. It's Asher. You could have given me a warning."

"He and Corinne showed up at my office. I thought I was letting you off the hook by making up that shit about you being out of town...sparing you a night with me."

"Look how that turned out for me."

He lifts his chin. "You've got my number. Next time you want to bring a girl here, just text me and I'll know not to come."

I gauge him. "You'd probably race me here," I say, but we both know I don't really believe that.

He lets out a sigh. "Is it really that bad having to stomach me for a couple of hours? You used to spend time with me voluntarily."

"Until you had to fuck it all up."

He stares at me like he has shit to say but isn't gonna. "Fuck it. Quit asking if anyone wants another drink, and I'll get us out of here as soon as I see an opening, okay?"

"Fine," I say. He starts to walk away, but I say, "So you and Bailey now?"

He stops and turns to me. "Are you laying claim on her, too? One at a time, Hargrove. That's all I'm gonna let you have." He winks at me like the fucker he is and then heads back over to where everyone is hanging on the floor.

When we rejoin the group, Corrine and Asher regale us with the story of how Asher proposed, and Bailey and Kylie ask questions about the wedding planning. I wonder if this is painful for Kylie. She did just plan a wedding, after all. As I listen, I try to imagine Kylie walking down the aisle with some strange guy waiting for her at the end. It's almost inconceivable to me.

Jack stands up. "I'm over the whole boat thing. Let's go get some food." He gives me a contrite look, and I hate that I'm not despising him this evening.

"All right," Asher says, pulling Corinne to him. "Come on, baby. I'll get you some steak nachos."

She lowers her chin. "With jalapenos and black olives?"

"With whatever you want on them, sweetness." He stands and helps her up.

They all head for the door, and I meet Kylie's gaze. It's her move whether we stay or go. I don't want to influence her, but I really want to stay.

She looks down at her can of seltzer drink, moving her finger around the rim.

Jack and Bailey are out the door, and Asher is guiding Corinne that way when he turns around and sees we're not getting up.

He smiles at me, then holds up his hand. "Good to see you, man."

"Yep," I say.

"Nice to meet you, Kylie," he says with a big smile.

"Nice to meet you both."

Corinne nods with a smile as Asher ushers her off the boat and then shuts the door behind him.

Kylie meets my gaze. "Quick, lock it."

I smile and then get up and walk over there, doing just that.

She giggles. "I was joking."

"I'm not. I should have had it locked to begin with. I would have if I didn't think it would creep you out."

She stands up, straightening out the backs of her shorts. "I'm not creeped out by you, Brett."

My name on her lips triggers my smile. "Good."

"Besides, wouldn't Jack have just unlocked the door and come right in? I assume he has a key, too."

I let out a hard breath and put my hands on her hips. "Can we not talk about him tonight, or ever again?"

She gives me a knowing smile. "Come on, you didn't hate him being here tonight nearly as much as you'd like to think you did."

I just shake my head, glancing around.

"I watched you when he made jokes...a few inside ones, I'm guessing. You two were friends once."

"Once," I say.

"I think you stay mad at him out of loyalty to Tori."

I don't respond.

She smiles. "That's sweet. Family first, right?"

I pull her closer to me. "Can we please change the subject now?"

"Sure thing. What subject would you like to discuss? The national debt? The ecosystem?"

I shut her up with a kiss, and the anticipation of the past couple of hours is instantly satisfied. As I run my hands up her back, she slides hers down to my ass, and her attitude about what she wants to happen on this boat tonight seems to have changed. She steps backwards, pulling us apart, and takes my hand, tugging me toward the bed. She glances at it. "Can we?"

"We can do whatever you want," I say.

"I haven't decided what I want yet. Is that okay?" she asks.

"Fine by me. I'll be standing by."

We climb onto the bed and start kissing again, this time with more intensity than I was expecting from her. She hikes her long leg over mine, and our bodies line up, mine lit up like a Roman candle.

My hands are in her hair and on her back, and I'm trying to respect her wishes and let her lead us, but I'm not at all used to this. Typically, when I lie down with a girl, we're both all-in, and there're no questions about where the night is going. But she's made it clear she's not ready to commit to anything in this bed, so I'm being as good as a choirboy.

She presses her pelvis against mine, and my cock can no longer stand down. She moves my hand from her lower back to her ass, and I grab it, crushing her body against mine. She breathes against my mouth, letting out a moan that threatens to send me over the edge.

"Fuck, Kylie," I whisper.

She directs my hand to her zipper, pressing it against her. "Touch me," she says.

She doesn't have to tell me twice. I'm in her shorts in half a second, and my body sizzles when I touch her. She presses up against me, her face buried in my neck and her hand gripping my shoulder. She groans, blowing heat against my neck, and it's all I can do to keep myself in check. She grips me harder, panting into my ear and then holding her breath until she finally lets out a wail that has me grinning with pride at how quick and easy it was to set her free like that.

She kisses my neck, making her way to my mouth, running her fingers through my hair. We're both salty from sweat and the heat between us. She kisses me for a while, and it's so right—slower than before since she's let off some steam. I try to settle myself down, but my dick isn't cooperating.

She undoes each of the buttons on my shirt as our mouths are occupied and then pushes it to either side of me, moving down, kissing my neck, my collarbone, my chest, my abs... I'm trying not to get my hopes up, but the way she's moving, slowly down south, my heart rate spikes.

She undoes my button and zipper, pulling down my shorts, and then takes me into her mouth. I close my eyes, my body spiking with a heat surge as I settle into the sensations she's giving me. I can usually think about something funky to make it last longer, but I don't want to hold back with her. It feels too good.

The buildup is relentless, and it's happening now, so I push her head away but she grips me, finishing me off. I stare at the ceiling, arm draped across my chest, catching my breath as she crawls up my body, finding a place beside me. I meet her gaze, my heartbeat slowly on the decline. "That was unexpected."

"You're welcome."

I put my hand behind my head, and she drapes herself across me. With other girls, this kind of move would feel like suffocation. But right now, all I experience is contentment.

I run my hand over her back. "Is it weird for you hearing about Asher and Corinne's wedding?"

"No, why would that be weird?"

"I know you were supposed to be getting married, right? Weren't you planning your wedding?"

She lets out a sigh. "I was, but now that I'm disengaged from the situation, I wonder if I was ever really going to go through with it."

"What makes you say that?"

"I don't know. There's a big difference between a wedding and a marriage. I think a lot of brides get caught up in the wedding planning not realizing what the actual marriage is going to be like. I definitely fell into that category. It just seemed like something I had to do—like a logical next step. All my friends were married—every single one of them. I was the final holdout. But thinking back on it now, the whole thing was a blessing in disguise."

"Do you ever wish you had your old life back? Not the cheating asshole, but the rest of it."

"No. I really don't. It was an easy life, but it came with a price. I was beholden to my dad. Anything he wanted or needed from me he got—a new suit, a hostess for one of his many parties, even a lunch date. I would drop everything for him. I wasn't his daughter, I was his personal assistant, available twenty-four seven. I think that's part of why he's so upset that I left. Who's going to do his bidding now?"

"Is he married?"

"No, not since my mom left when I was sixteen. But why would he need to be married with me around taking care of all his shit all the time?"

I frown. "I didn't know your mom left. Where did she go?"

She rolls off of me and lies on her side. "California. It's fine. Old news."

I rub her arm. "I'm sorry."

She forces a smile, but it's not all the way there. "Don't feel bad for me. I've led a really privileged life."

I don't reply, but it strikes me how lucky I've been to have my family close to me all these years, warts and all.

Her eyes droop closed. "I think the week is winning. I'm not sure how much longer I can stay awake."

"Ever slept on a boat?" I ask.

"Nope," she says with a lazy smile. "But there's a first time for everything."

I kiss her on the lips and then pull her close.

20

KYLIE

As I tiptoe back from the bathroom, I take a moment to pause and appreciate Brett's body. His shirt has fallen to either side, exposing his chest and abs, and his shorts have ridden down, giving me a glorious peek of that little patch of hair on his lower torso that leads south.

Part of me can't believe that I got to have him for the night and didn't take full advantage. I just wasn't ready yet. I needed to keep some control. I hadn't planned to take things as far as I did, but there was something empowering about going down on him. I enjoyed it for the first time in a long time.

He's so crazy different from Joshua. He's all man, through and through. So much game. He touches me and my bones go limp inside my body. It's like when I touch still water and ripples form all around my finger. That's my body when Brett touches me.

I'm about to slide back into bed with him when his phone rings, rustling him. He pats the bed and then his pants pockets.

I find it at the foot of the bed and hand it to him.

"Thanks," he says, squinting as the sun peeps through a closed curtain. "Hello?"

Whatever the person on the other end of that line says has him wide awake. "I'll be right there."

He ends the call and darts out of bed. "We've got to go."

"What's going on?"

"My grandmother's missing." He looks around at the empty cans and bottles. "I'll have to come back and clean this later."

I grab my purse and step outside onto the dock as he locks the door behind us. He runs his hand through his hair as we practically jog to the car. "I don't have time to take you home."

"That's fine. I can help."

He glances over at me as we speed walk toward the car. But he doesn't say anything.

"Or I can get a rideshare?" I ask, feeling completely displaced.

He seems to consider this, but I'm really hoping he doesn't take me up on this offer, because the credit card I had in my app no longer works.

"No, you can just come with me if you don't mind."

"No, of course not."

We jump into the car and drive Northbound without a word. He's laser-focused on the road, and it looks like he could crush nails with his teeth. I want to say something, but I have no clue what. He doesn't exactly seem receptive, understandably.

We pull into a community with small homes, paint chipping off the sides and grass and weeds grown up beside several of them. He parks in front of a trailer that has a couple of cars already parked there.

We both get out and Brett heads inside. I'm not sure if I should follow him or not, so I hang back.

A guy in his late teens resembling Brett but a little shorter and with more of a baby face approaches. When he looks up from his phone and sees me, he freezes and then looks away.

"Hi, I'm Kylie," I say, my voice shaky.

"Hi," he says with a forced wave, still looking away from me.

"I'm Brett's friend," I say.

He just nods, looking anywhere but at me.

Brett comes out. "What happened?"

"I guess I forgot to put the padlock on the door when I got home last night," the guy says, running his hand through his hair just like Brett does when something is off.

"Dammit, Matthew. You've got to start thinking."

"I just fucking forgot once, okay?"

"Once is all it takes."

The guy scrunches up his face and grabs a handful of his hair like he's going to pull it out of his head. Brett closes his eyes like he's recalibrating. "I'm sorry. Let's just find her. Have you knocked on any of the neighbors' doors to see if they've seen her?"

"No," the guy says almost desperately.

"What have you been doing?"

"I've just been walking around and looking for her. What the hell do you think I've been doing?"

"All right, you go look down by the street and I'm gonna start knocking on doors. One of us should stay here in case she comes back." Brett looks at me.

"I'll stay here," I say.

They both take off in different directions and I exhale a breath for the first time. Brett bangs on the door of the trailer next to this one, and an irritated man comes to the door, shakes his head, and then shuts the door in Brett's face. Brett tries another and then another, until he's out of my sight.

A woman walks up in an oversized, ratty Guns N' Roses T-shirt. I can't tell if she's wearing shorts or not. She pops a cigarette into her mouth and lights it, blowing the smoke in my direction. She's oddly familiar to me, but I can't figure out why until she opens her mouth. "What the fuck is going on around here?"

My heartbeat pauses as I realize this has got to be Tori's mother. Her low, throaty voice is identical to Tori's. She looks like Tori, too, but she's much thinner, and not in a healthy way.

"Their grandmother is missing," I say.

"Mmm," she utters, glancing around. "That's what they get for keeping her here. If it was my mom, I'd put her in a home." She looks me up and down like I'm pond scum. "Who are you?"

I don't want to answer. I want her to walk away. "I'm just a friend."

She smirks. "Yeah, I know all about Brett's friends. Don't get too attached, honey." She takes another puff and then walks to a nearby trailer and goes inside. With this one conversation, I understand more about Tori than I ever imagined I would.

I stand outside the door, pacing for what seems like hours until Brett finally shows up. "The police have her. They're bringing her and my mom back now."

I put my hand to my heart. "Thank God."

He nods, glancing around, looking completely shaken.

I put my hand on his arm, but he tugs it away. "It's fine."

With that, I am completely shut off. "You can wait in the car if you'd like," he says, handing me the keys.

I take this as a directive and get in his car. It's not long before a police car pulls up and a middle-aged woman gets out of the car then helps an elderly woman out. The two women go inside while Brett talks to the cop. The teenager, who I assume is Brett's little brother, kicks dirt around, not looking the police officer in the eye.

When the cop finally gets in his car and leaves, Brett talks to his brother, who doesn't seem to have a problem looking Brett in the eye. After a while of them bickering back and forth, Brett goes inside, but his brother walks away.

It's a while before Brett comes out, looking like he has run a marathon. He glances around, and when he makes eye contact with me in the car, it seems like he's just now remembering I'm here. He walks over to my door. I've already got the window rolled down. It wasn't that hot out here when all this started, but the sun has definitely come out, and it's burning up in here.

"I meant for you to run the AC," he says. "That's why I gave you the keys."

"I'm fine. How's your grandmother?"

"She's okay. Just got disoriented. Have you seen my brother?"

I point. "He went that way."

He follows my gaze and then says, "I won't be that much longer."

"Take your time. Seriously."

He forces a half-hearted smile and walks away.

I finally break down and turn the car and air conditioner on. I want to go in and introduce myself to Brett's mother and grandmother, but this definitely does not seem like the appropriate time. After a while, Brett gets back with his brother in tow. His brother goes inside without another word, and Brett gets in the car.

"Listen," I say, "if you need to stay, I can call someone to come get me."

"We're an hour away. I just need to take you home."

I want to press the matter, but it doesn't seem like I should push him right now. He backs out and we head home, riding in silence for a long time. I can't take it any longer, so I say, "I assume that was your brother."

"Yeah. That's not how I meant for you to meet him."

"I noticed he wouldn't really look at me."

"He's like that with strangers."

I try not to let his words sting, but it's a little tough. He's not in a great mood right now, and his tone reflects it, so I keep my thoughts to myself. He knows I'm here if he'd like to talk.

When we arrive at his place, he parks the car in his driveway, and I wonder if he's going to invite me in. "I'll go with you to Tori's house. I want to talk to her a minute."

"Sure," I say, as if he was asking and not telling.

We walk into Tori's unit, but she's not home. I turn to him. "I guess she's gone."

"I'm gonna go home. I'm sorry about today. I know I hijacked your whole day."

"It's totally fine. I'm just glad your grandma is okay."

He nods and turns to walk out the door, barely giving me a wave.

I take a shower and get dressed. I eat something, do a load of laundry, and then check in with Samantha, who I haven't had a proper conversation with since I got here. I leave everything about Brett out. There's no need for anyone back home to know about him or my feelings for him. Not that I don't trust Samantha, but it's just better for me to keep my mouth shut.

I try to watch television, but I'm too anxious. I feel so displaced, like I'm living someone else's life. If I can ever get my own space, I'm hoping I will start to feel more like a real Florida resident. But for now, I'm a homeless person who strangers have taken pity on.

My phone rings, an actual call. It's my mom. I close my eyes out of exhaustion. If ever there was a convenient time to talk to her, it's now. Though I'd rather be struck by lightning.

I answer it. "Hey."

"Finally, you take my call. I only gave birth to you."

"Yes, I know. What's up?"

"I'm just checking on you. I hear you've moved to Florida," she says with a laugh.

"Just like I said I was going to," I say.

"Yeah, but I didn't believe you'd really do it."

"Hmm," I utter, because I don't have anything else to say to her.

"You could've come out here to California," she says.

"You could've offered that when I talked to you a few weeks ago."

"Well, it wouldn't be necessarily convenient for you to come here and live with me, but you're my daughter. It's not like I'd let you go homeless."

I roll my eyes. My mom moved to California when I was sixteen. I would visit her for a week every summer, and I could tell she was done with me after about two or three days. We'd spend the rest of the week in our own pockets of her mansion...or her husband of the week's mansion, I should say. If I'd have gone to her now, I have no reason to think it'd be any different.

"I'm not homeless," I lie.

"Well, that's a relief. So what are you gonna do down there in Florida?"

"I've got a job, actually."

"Doing what?" she says, like it's the craziest idea she's ever heard.

"I'm working at a resort."

"Like bringing people mai tais?"

I roll my eyes. This is what my mom thinks resort workers do.

"I'm cleaning houses, actually," I say, just to get her goat.

"When you're up for having an adult conversation, feel free to call me back."

"Yep," I say, and we hang up.

TORI FINALLY GETS HOME late in the afternoon wearing the same clothes she had on when she left for her date last night. I see I'm not the only one who didn't come home.

"Looks like you had a good night," I say.

"It was unexpected," she says, but her smile reveals everything. "I'm gonna jump in the shower."

"Cool. Um, did Brett get in touch with you?"

"Yeah," she says, offering no further info.

After she gets out, she comes into the living room with a silk robe on and wet hair combed out down her back. I'm surprised at how long her hair is. She always wears it up in a bun, so I've never really been able to tell.

"I heard you met Brett's family today," she says, not looking up from her phone as she sits in the armchair.

I want to say I didn't actually meet them, but instead, I say, "I think I might have met your mom."

She huffs a laugh. "I bet that was a barrel of laughs."

I don't know how to respond to that. I could tell her I know what it's like to have a mom who you don't see eye to eye with, but the last thing I want to do right now is talk about my mom.

We sit in silence, scrolling through our phones, until a knock sounds at the door. She stands. "That's Brett."

I sit in somewhat stunned silence as she answers the door in that silk robe. He comes in. "Hey," he says to me.

"Hey," I say, not sure what's happening, until the two of them head toward her bedroom. A moment later, the door closes, and I'm left glancing around the living room, looking for invisible answers.

After a few minutes of being glued to my seat, I realize I need to move my butt out of here. I walk out to the front porch and sit in a chair, glancing through my phone, but the battery is starting to get low, so I finally just put it down and sit there staring at the street, wondering what the hell is going on in there.

I have to understand that the two of them are like brother and sister and this is just what they do. But I want to be the one he talks things through with.

I've been sitting here for at least twenty minutes when a group walks past on the sidewalk. It's Bailey and Simone and a couple of guys. I squint and notice that one of the guys is Jack.

"Hey," Bailey shouts. "What's going on?"

"Oh, nothing," I say as I glance at the doorway and then look back at them, feeling completely out of place.

"Come with us," Simone says. "We're going to the Circle."

Part of me thinks I should, just to get out of Brett and

Tori's way, but the other part wants to know what the hell is going on. "I'm okay, but thanks for asking."

They wave and walk off, but in a moment, Jack comes up the steps toward me. "What's going on?"

I force a smile. "Nothing. I'm just sitting here."

"Mmm-hmm. Now do you want to tell me what's really going on?" He pulls up the empty chair next to me.

I glance at the house. "Are you supposed to be here?"

"Most definitely not." He nudges me on the knee. "You don't seem okay. Talk to me."

I look through the window at the bedroom door, which remains irritatingly closed. I give him the short version about the day and then say, "I guess he wanted to talk to Tori about something to do with it all."

"Let me give you a word to the wise. Anybody who wants to date either one of them has to be really okay with what they've got going on. I'll be honest, I couldn't handle it."

"Is that what happened between Tori and you?"

He smiles. "If you wanted to know, all you had to do was ask."

My neck heats up. "I'm sorry, I guess I got caught up in the rumor mill."

"You really don't have to worry about the two of them hooking up or anything."

"I believe that," I say, failing to mention she's in there in a bathrobe. "But is this what it's like? When there's a problem, he goes to Tori and not the person he's dating?"

He considers me with a smile. "Come to the Circle with us. Just step away for a minute. When this is blown over, you can talk to him about how you feel, and then maybe he'll come to you next time."

His words make perfect sense. But I certainly don't want

to mess things up by hanging with Jack when I was supposed to be waiting for Brett.

A car pulls up, and Janelle opens the passenger door and then slams it shut. Shouldering a tote bag, she marches up the steps and seems not to notice us until she's opening the front door. She looks Jack up and down. "What the hell are you doing here?"

"Just leaving."

She glances between Jack and me. "What's going on between you two?"

I sit up straight like a teacher has scolded me. "I'm just waiting for Brett. He's inside with Tori."

She gives me a skeptical look, shakes her head, and then goes inside.

I meet Jack's gaze. "I think I'll take you up on that night out."

"Yep."

21

KYLIE

The Circle is a really fun place filled with bars, restaurants, and carnival games, all surrounding a lake in the center. People wait in line to strap themselves into a harness and zip-line across the water while kids jump on a mega trampoline that skyrockets them into the air. It's family-oriented and a little cheesy, but I like it.

In the course of about two hours, we have hit three bars, and Jack won a huge stuffed animal that he offered to any of us girls who wanted it. We all knew to step back and let Bailey have that one.

I keep checking my phone, but there's no messages from Brett, which really starts to irk me. He has to know by now that I left, but it looks like he doesn't care. It would be fine if he wouldn't have said all that stuff to me last night about his feelings for me. I'm starting to wonder if I didn't fall into the same trap a thousand girls have fallen into before me.

Simone and Bailey are out on the dance floor putting on a show. I'm not quite in the mood to be a girl sandwich, so I stand at the table, nursing a beer, which is not helping my strained heart. Jack comes back from the bar with a bottle of water. It hasn't gotten past me that he's not had a single alcoholic drink tonight.

He glances down at my phone. "Nothing from Mr. Right?"

I shake my head and drag my gaze to meet his.

He pulls me into his chest, and I've got to admit, it feels good there. Jack is a really tall hunk of a guy. And he's nice on top of that. It's comforting to be in what feels like a safe space for a moment.

I pull back from him. "Do you ever just feel defeated?"

He nods. "Yep. I do."

"Last night was really great. I mean after you left, and actually, before that, too. It was good when you were there but..." I stop before I make this any worse.

"I know what you mean," he says.

"And then things change like this." I snap my fingers. "Not to mention what happened with Janelle earlier. I was only supposed to be staying with Tori because she was back with Chris. I don't even know what's gonna happen when I go back there tonight. I'm hoping Bailey and Simone will let me crash on their couch." I glance at the dance floor and realize they're gone. "Where are they, by the way?"

Jack looks around. "I don't know. They were on the dance floor a minute ago. Maybe they're in the restroom."

Easton, who has been hanging with us, steps up to the table. "They left."

My chest fills with panic. I really was planning to ask them if I could crash on their couch. I can't imagine going back to Tori's right now with Janelle as pissed as she was.

"Are you sure? Maybe they're in the bathroom," I say out of desperation.

"No, they're gone. In fact, I think Bailey said something about hoping Jack would fuck completely off."

Jack pinches the bridge of his nose. "Shit."

"What did you do to her?" Easton asks.

"I don't know. She might have been pissed that I was hugging Kylie before."

I wince. "Really? You think that would set her off that easily?" I ask Jack.

"I didn't want to say anything, but I saw her look at us, and the expression on her face wasn't good."

"Crap," I say, imagining the situation from her point of view. She doesn't know me that well. For all she knew, that was my way of going for Jack the second things went sour with Brett. I look up at Jack. "I swear, I wasn't—"

He waves me off. "I know you weren't. I wasn't either."

Easton holds out his hand to Jack. "I'm out, too, man. See you Monday. Good to meet you, Kylie."

I force a smile and a wave.

Jack bites his lip, looking around. "I wish I wasn't such a fuckup all the time."

"Actually, this one is all my fault."

"I like Bailey, a lot. But we aren't together. I haven't even kissed her or anything."

"So you know she's into you?"

He gives me a look. "It's kind of hard not to notice. I liked hanging with her last night and thought I'd try again tonight in another group, but it's just not happening for me. I'm not trying to hurt her."

I squeeze his forearm. "You're allowed to hang with people to see if there's a spark. You haven't done anything wrong."

"I still feel like an asshole."

"You're an asshole, and I'm homeless again. We're not a good duo."

"I know how this is gonna sound, but you're more than welcome to stay at my place tonight." He tosses up both hands. "A hundred percent platonically. I've got a spare bedroom. Clean sheets on the bed and everything. It's all yours."

I remember Janelle and how pissed she looked at me. I think of Brett and how he has still not sent me a text since he walked into that room with Tori and shut the door. The idea of going back to that street makes my stomach swirl. "Are you absolutely sure you don't mind?"

He picks up his water bottle. "I'll take us home."

22

KYLIE

When I wake up, I'm completely disoriented. I wonder if I've stepped into a Restoration Hardware showroom. With a jolt and a sickening in my gut, I remember I'm at Jack's condo.

Not that there's anything wrong with Jack or his condo. Both are lovely. But I slept here. Being temporarily homeless, I have very few options, but this can't be good for whatever I have going on with Brett.

I find my purse in the bed with me and fish my phone out to see if he's called, but it's completely dead. I really should've found a charger last night, but I was too irritated and too fluffy to care if Brett texted or not. I definitely care now.

I go to the bathroom and check myself. I haven't looked this rough in a while, with makeup dragging down my face and my hair frizzy and tangled. My looks match the way I feel perfectly.

I clean myself up and then open the door to the bedroom to find Jack sitting at his kitchen table with a mug of something and a tablet.

He looks up at me. "Hey. I was about to come and check for proof of life."

I put my hand to my forehead. "My phone died. What time is it?"

"Ten fifteen."

I slide into a chair at the table with him. "I'm so sorry. I feel like such an idiot. I can't believe you've had to sit here all morning while I slept the day away."

"I've just been up a couple of hours. I've actually been getting caught up on some work."

"Do you ever stop working?"

"It's not like I have anything else to do," he says with a smile, but the smile doesn't reach his eyes. "I don't drink coffee, but I can make you a green tea?" he asks.

"You're one of those healthy people, huh?" I ask, but it wasn't so long ago that I was one, too.

This makes him chuckle. "I guess you could call me that. I have fruit, too, if you'd like some."

This is where I need to refuse the offer and get out of his hair, but in my financial state, I will take any food that's offered to me right now. "That would be great. Do you have a charger I can borrow?"

"Sure," he says and brings me one.

I put my phone on the charger and then meet Jack at the table, where he gives me a bowl of pineapple, strawberry, blueberries, and mango. He sets down a container of yogurt and a box of granola, and I feel like my old self—the good parts of my old self, that is.

"How are you not married yet?" I ask him.

He sits down at the table. "You and my mom share the same concern."

"I'm serious. You're an eligible bachelor. This place is

impeccably decorated, you're healthy, you've got a great job, and look at you."

He lifts one eyebrow.

"Oh, please. You know you're gorgeous."

"Are you interested?"

I glance up at him and then look down at my bowl. "I'm way more intrigued by this breakfast right now."

"That's what I thought." He goes back to his tablet, and I feel like we're an old married couple who has lost interest in sex.

We sit together in comfortable silence while I eat way too much, and he types into his tablet with furrowed brows. After I finish, I take my dishes to the sink and then pick up my phone, which has charged enough for me to check it. My heart swells when I see Brett's name in a text.

I'm sorry about yesterday. I'd like to talk to you. Are you up?

"Shit," I say under my breath.

Jack looks up at me. "You okay?"

"Yeah, I'm good. Just finally heard from him."

"And?"

"He's apologizing for last night."

"That's good, right?"

I toss up my hand. "What about me? I slept here last night."

"Yeah, *slept* being the operative word."

"He won't understand that," I say.

"Fuck him if he doesn't."

"Oh, so you would be cool with it if you were him in this situation?"

"I've been him in this situation, and it didn't go so well, come to think of it."

I toss up my hands.

"Just don't tell him," he says.

"I don't want to start off this thing with him on a lie."

"You know you did nothing wrong. If you make some confession to him, you're just going to seem guilty. It's all innocent. There's nothing to see here. If it were me, I'd leave it at that." He puts his tablet down. "Have you thought about where you're going to live?"

I rub my temple. "I'm hoping on a wing and a prayer that Janelle and her boyfriend will get back together."

He stands up. "If they don't, you know you're welcome to stay here."

I hate to even entertain this thought, but I think I'm just that desperate. "Are you serious?"

"It wouldn't bother me."

"What if you wanted to bring a girl back here?"

He walks over to the bar in the kitchen, picking up his wallet and keys. "That's not my thing."

"Girls aren't your thing?"

"Sleeping around. I guess I'm a serial monogamist that way."

"What if you start dating someone?"

"That's not going to happen either."

"It could."

"Not right now. I guess I'm still hung up on someone I can't have."

From what I keep hearing, it sounds to me like he's talking about Tori. My heart stings for him. Love is so fragile and powerful at the same time.

We head out and Jack drives me to Tori's unit. As we pull up, my heart pounds when I see Brett sitting on his front porch.

"He's been waiting for you," Jack says.

Brett simply glares at the car and then walks inside. I

pinch the bridge of my nose, trying to figure out how this weekend has taken such a disastrous turn.

"Do you need me to wait?" Jack asks.

I let out a sigh. "No, I have my car."

"You know where I live."

I consider him. "Why are you being so nice to me?"

"To be honest, you kind of seem like a little sister to me. I hope that doesn't offend you."

I manage a smile, because I really appreciate him right now. "Most definitely not."

I head up the steps and knock on the door. Tori opens it and greets me with a frigid gaze. Janelle sits on the couch, wiping her eyes. She gathers her knees to her chest and won't look at me. I remember Tori saying my staying there would be a different story if Janelle were back home. There's no question of what my next move needs to be.

"I'll just grab my bag," I say.

Tori simply opens the door farther and walks away from me, finding her place next to Janelle on the couch.

I SIT in my car in the parking lot of the public beach access, charging my phone. I text Bailey.

Hey, what's up? You left kind of early last night.

No response. I can't believe I've somehow managed to lose Brett, Tori, and Bailey in one fell swoop of a night. With the distance I've put between myself and my old life, I truly feel like I have no one.

I flip through Instagram, looking at pictures of my former circle of friends—the couples Joshua and I spent most all of our social time with. Life has gone on for them— at least the three remaining couples. I don't see Jillian and

Bryce there, or Joshua, for that matter. I wonder if he and Jillian are still screwing or if the thrill of it all is gone since their secret is out in the open now. It's crazy to say, but part of me feels a little sorry for Jillian. This friend group was her life. She's probably somewhere tearing up at this picture of her friends having fun without her.

I toss my phone in the passenger seat and stare into the horizon, unable to believe I'm in this beautiful place but in such a dark corner on the inside. As conflicted as I am about it, I drive to Jack's place. I text him from the parking lot, and he buzzes me in. When he opens the door for me, I say, "Are you absolutely a hundred percent sure about this?"

"Do you have any other choice?" he says.

I think about that for a long moment and then follow him inside.

23

BRETT

My plan to forget about Kylie is a bust. I went to my mom's on Tuesday night, and when I showed up again on Wednesday night, she practically kicked me out, saying she was too tired to make conversation with me. She basically told me not to come back till Sunday.

I can't believe Jack fucking Massey dropped Kylie off last Sunday morning. My mind has been cluttered with images of what could have happened with them Saturday night. It's almost hard to buy that she would give herself to him after being with me the night before. But I can't deny the expression of sheer guilt on her face when she saw me. He even looked almost contrite.

Tori leans against the doorframe of my office. "You gonna be working late?"

I check the clock on the wall. "I've got a four o'clock."

"Not anymore. Parents just picked him up."

"Seriously?"

"Don't look so disappointed. Just means we can get something to eat before we go out later."

"I'm not going out tonight."

"Yeah you are. I'm tired of your mopey ass this week."

I walk around, picking up my room. "I would think you'd be as pissed as I am."

"Why, because Kylie's staying with Jack?"

I eye her. "You know that for a fact?"

"Confirmed it earlier today. I had lunch at the bar with Logan."

"How does Logan know?"

"He's a bartender. He listens for a living."

I toss a tub of putty into the crate a little too hard.

Tori rolls her eyes. "Jack swears nothing's happening." She puts air quotes around the words. "This is according to Easton, who was at the bar having a beer last night, chatting Logan up."

"This place is as gossipy as a barber shop."

"Come on. That bowl of tortilla soup I had at noon has faded."

"I think I'll stay here and get caught up on some continuing education."

"That's not much of a Friday night," comes Robert's voice from the doorway.

"Hey, man," I say. "What are you doing here?"

"You two are just the people I've come here to see. I was hoping I could talk you both into coming over for dinner tonight. I know you probably have plans later but I'm talking early. Like six o'clock?"

Tori shrugs. "Okay."

"I've met someone," Robert says with a smile.

This takes me completely off guard. "Seriously?"

"Her name is Catherine. She teaches high school English."

"How did you meet her?" Tori asks.

He lowers his chin. "Online. Don't judge."

"You do know that's how people meet these days, right?" Tori says.

"I know. It's just that it's my first time meeting someone this way. But I think it's working out okay."

"That's great," I say, realizing I need to say something. I've just never known Robert to settle into a relationship.

"Can you make it?" Robert asks.

"Yeah, of course," I say.

"What can we bring?" Tori asks.

"Just bring yourselves. See you in"—he looks at his watch—"a couple of hours?"

"Yep," Tori says, then Robert's out. After he's down the hall, Tori and I look at each other, and she shrugs. "At least somebody's getting laid."

Tori and I stop and get a bottle of wine, though neither of us drinks it or knows really what to get. We've been to dinner at Robert's house a few times, but we never seem to remember to find out what kind of wine to get. Tori says we don't want to know, because it would be more than we could afford.

When we pull up in the driveway, my stomach turns as I see Jack fucking Massey's car sitting there. "I should've fucking known."

"Come on, teacher's pet. Share the glory."

I meet her gaze. "Are you okay with this?"

"Like I have a choice. The boss has invited us to his house. Do you think I'm gonna act like a child and say I can't be in the same room with a guy I dated for less than a month?"

I exhale a deep breath. I have no idea if Robert knows that Jack and I can't stand each other. He probably does, but it's not like he would make any concessions for us, or that I would want him to.

We head up the sidewalk, dread bearing down on me with each step. I ring the bell, and Robert answers the door, smiling like a sucker in love. "Come on in."

We follow Robert into the kitchen, where a woman around his age stands at the stove, stirring something. Jack and Kylie sit at the bar facing the woman, who is talking a hundred miles a minute.

I meet Kylie's gaze, and she gives me a nervous smile. I look away and focus on the lady at the stove, a rope tightening around my heart.

"Catherine," Robert says, "I'd like you to meet Brett and Tori. They both work at Kids Company. Brett's an OT and Tori's a recreational therapist."

"It is so nice to meet you both. Robert talks about you guys and Jack all the time." She looks over at Jack and then back at me like she's doting on children.

Catherine launches into a narrative about what she's making for dinner and where she got the recipe, and I nod, my whole body fueling up like a gas tank on fire. I'm not even looking at Kylie or Jack, but feeling their presence together right here, inches away, taunts me like a massive *fuck you.*

Robert takes the bottle of wine from Tori and says, "This is a great brand. Look, Catherine, it's a Pinot Noir. We had this one last week."

"Yes, we love that one," Catherine says, handing him a corkscrew.

"I'll pour everyone a glass," Robert says.

"I'm good," Jack says, "but thanks."

Motherfucker's too good for my wine, huh?

"Why don't you four head out to the patio, and we'll be there in just a minute with the wine and some appetizers," Robert says.

We all play along, padding to the patio. Once we get out there, no one sits. We all just mill around awkwardly.

Tori pulls out her phone and starts flipping through it. Jack follows suit. I start to pull my phone out, but Kylie says, "Can we please talk just a minute?"

"We won't listen," Tori says, not looking up from her phone.

I glance at Jack, but he's completely engrossed in his phone, frowning and typing into it like he's working.

"This isn't the place," I say.

"Please. You can show me the pool," she says, pointing at it.

I glance at Tori, I guess for some sort of permission. I don't want to leave her alone with Jack. I know she can handle herself, but I also know being alone with him can't be comfortable for her.

Not looking up from her phone, she gives me a shooing motion. I roll my eyes and walk down the steps toward the pool.

When we get far enough away that no one can hear, I stop and face Kylie, but I don't look at her.

"I tried to text you a dozen times this week," she says. "Well, not a dozen, but probably like five or six at least."

I just look at the pool.

"Nothing has happened between Jack and me."

I dare to meet her gaze, looking for truth in her eyes, and I find it there—that or else she's a good actress. "Like the same way nothing happened between us on the boat last

Friday night?" It's a cheap shot, but she's not getting away with this so easily.

She looks down, frustrated, and then meets my gaze. "I have been staying with him, but what other options do I have? I texted Bailey, but she's pissed at me, too."

The fact that Bailey's mad only gives legitimacy to my biggest concerns. I want to bolt, but I'm stuck here at Robert's house, where I have to play nice.

"I really don't know why she's so upset," Kylie says. "I suspect she might have seen Jack and me talking, or maybe hugging at the bar on Saturday night, but she's totally off base."

I shift uneasily, glancing at the house, hoping Robert will save me with hors d'oeuvres. "I don't want to hear this."

"I was upset. I was available to you all day, but you ignored me, waiting for Tori to get home. Then when you got there, you closed the door to Tori's bedroom. What was I supposed to think about that?"

"Tori closed that door."

"But you didn't open it back up." She lowers her voice. "She was in a silk robe."

"You know Tori and I aren't like that."

"Yeah, but did you see her in that thing?"

I wince. "I don't think of her that way."

She sighs. "I believe that. But what about the way you ran to her to figure stuff out when I was right there in the car with you for an hour and you were totally quiet? Is that what a relationship with you would look like? Anytime you needed to talk about anything, I would step aside for Tori?"

"No, of course not. It's just that she knows all the history."

"Tell me the history."

I can feel myself conceding to her, as much as my brain is telling me not to. "Okay, I'll admit that I screwed up. But the fact that you left with Jack Massey without even texting me was not fucking cool."

"I know. I was upset, and I should've told you where I was going. Is there any way we can get past this?"

"Are you still living with him?"

She closes her mouth and her eyes give me my answer.

I huff a humorless laugh.

"What are my options? I'm on the wait list for housing. I'm saving every dime for first and last month's rent. I'm literally looking for anywhere to stay every day. I still have not gotten a paycheck yet. I hear it's going to be another week because of the way payroll works. I'm in survival mode and trying desperately to make this life work. If you can't handle this right now, and we need to just be friends, that's fine. But this is temporary. I'm not living with him as a couple. He told me I'm like a little sister to him."

"How classic."

"If he's so hot for me, why hasn't he tried to kiss me one single time? Or flirted with me? Why do we go to separate rooms every night?"

I consider her, wanting to cave, but my pride won't let me. "Why is he so damned willing to have you stay there? Have you thought of that?"

"I asked him that question. He's just being nice."

I shake my head.

"He's totally still in love with Tori. Any fool can see it." We both turn to look at them, and on cue, Jack glances up from his phone at Tori like a lovesick Saint Bernard.

I look at Kylie, the determination in her eyes, the hope, and I know I want everything she wants. Most of all, I want to quit feeling like I've lost everything. "How is this supposed to work? I'm gonna take you out on a date and then drop you off at his house?" I point at him for effect. "Are you kidding me?"

She looks away. "Then let's just be friends. I'd rather have your friendship than nothing."

As the next words are about to come out of my mouth, I feel Tori bearing down the weight of her stare on me even though she's still buried in her phone. "Stay with me."

Kylie shakes her head. "I'm sorry, but that's just not an option. This is brand-new. We're trying each other on right now. That first weekend was nice, but it had an expiration date. I don't know exactly how long it's going to take for me to get on my feet. I might need somewhere to stay for two or three months."

I nod, understanding where she's coming from, especially knowing how quickly things went south with Madison after we moved too fast. But I still cannot imagine myself dropping her off at his place.

"Why don't you go talk to Jack," she says. "Ask him what's going on with us. If anything were happening, you know he'd want to brag about it to you."

"That's for damn sure."

Catherine comes outside holding a tray, and Kylie and I meet each other's silent gaze and then head over to the table.

Kylie and I sit across from each other, Jack and Tori next to us. The tension is so thick you could bounce off it. Catherine thankfully uses her gift of gab to yap away endlessly through dinner, with Robert smiling at her like he's won the lottery.

Catherine stands, taking Tori's plate, and Tori gets up. "Let me get that."

"No, please, sit. Robert and I will clear these dishes and

bring dessert. Give us just a moment." The two of them leave the four of us out here in our awkward silence.

Kylie turns to Tori. "Will you please show me the bathroom?"

Tori stands, and Kylie and Jack exchange a significant look. Their connection with one another makes my skin crawl.

Once they're gone, Jack stares at me. "Come on, man. You know me better than that."

"I know payback for you would be sweet right now."

Jack sits back in his chair. "We both know I fucked things up with Tori. I was jealous—losing-my-mind jealous. I couldn't see any sense. All I could see was her with you."

"Even though we both told you it wasn't like that with us?"

"I didn't get it. Honestly, I think it'd still be hard for me if she and I would've worked things out. I'm admitting this to you because I want you to know I'm not pissed at you or trying to get you back for anything. I'm fucking jealous of you. I'll probably always be jealous of you. But I'm not out to hurt you, and I damn sure wouldn't want to use Kylie as a pawn in some stupid game."

I gauge him, knowing none of that was easy for him to admit. I want to believe him, but it's too hard.

"I'm asking you to trust me...like you once did," he says. "Can you do that?" Robert and Catherine come back out carrying plated desserts. Catherine sets one in front of Jack. "This looks really good, thank you."

I know Jack. He never eats sugar, but he's going to eat that dessert so he doesn't hurt Catherine's feelings. Maybe he's not the worst guy in the world.

When it's time to go, everyone says their goodbyes, and

Catherine and Robert walk us outside. Jack goes to the passenger side of his car and holds the door open for Kylie. She hesitates, giving me a hopeful look. I just stand there, not sure what to do, so she gets in the car with him.

24

KYLIE

"**D**o you want me to take you to his place?" Jack asks.

I check my phone for a text from Brett, but there isn't one. "No, I guess I've just got to give it time and see if he'll come around."

"He will."

I glance over at Jack, leaned back in his driver's seat. "I wish I shared your confidence." I stare out the window, my stomach in knots from the whole evening. As we pull up in the parking lot of Jack's condo, my phone dings. It's a text from Brett.

Can I come get you?

I could float out of the seat I'm so relieved. I look over at Jack with a smile. "He came around."

Jack rolls his eyes at me, but he's smiling a little. He puts the car in reverse. "I'll take you over there."

When we pull up in front of Brett's unit, he's sitting on the front porch. But this time, he doesn't go inside. He stands up, pocketing his hands, his shoulders rising and his chest getting bigger.

"Tell him he can stand down," Jack says. "I'm getting my ass home."

"Thank you, Jack," I say, wanting to give him a hug or a kiss on the cheek but not daring to. I get out of the car, and with each step I take toward Brett, my heart beats faster.

"Hey," he says, his face still hard to read.

"Hey," I say. He opens the door and lets me inside. I stand in the living room, gripping my purse with both hands.

He closes the door behind him, then takes the purse from me and sets it on the dining room table. I clutch my hands together and then pull them apart, not knowing what to do with them. This stupid skirt I'm wearing doesn't have pockets.

I glance around. "Is Val home?"

"No."

"Mmm," I utter, my insides warming at the idea of an empty house.

He moves toward me, putting his hands on my hips. "I'm sorry."

I swallow. "For what? I'm the one who should be sorry."

"I want to share things with you. I want to tell you the history."

I nod, my heart swelling.

He pulls me closer to him. "But right now, I just want to be with you in my bed. You can call the shots like you did last time. Okay?"

I nod, the pressure swelling behind my eyes.

He smiles and wipes a tear away with his thumb. "Don't cry."

I shake my head. "I'm sorry."

He brings me into his chest, one arm around my back, the other on top of my head, as he strokes my hair. His body pressed against mine is like a seventy-degree day after a snowstorm. He pulls away from me and takes my hand, leading me to his bedroom.

He closes the door behind him and comes over to me. With a single finger, he moves a stray hair out of my face. "I don't want to fight with you again."

I grab two handfuls of his shirt and say, "Me either." I'm afraid to look him in the eye for fear my whole body will melt like a lit candle.

He lifts my chin with his knuckle, and I'm forced to meet his gaze. He stares at me with those eyes that bring my body to life, and it's more than my libido can take.

"I want this," I say, my center so hot I could melt ice. "I want you."

"Are you sure?"

I nod. "I'm positive."

He kisses me, and I can barely stand up straight, my body having lost its ability to balance. I steady myself and pull away, focusing on undoing the buttons on his shirt. I smooth my hands over his shoulders as I slide the shirt down his arms. His tanned skin is so tempting I want to taste it. I trail kisses along his shoulder and his collarbone, my hands roaming down his strong back. When I come up for air, he slides his hands over my skirt and then grips my ass as he pulls me to him.

He walks us to the bed and rids me of my shirt before I collapse onto the mattress. He's still standing, and I'm right there, so I undo his shorts and loop my thumbs through the waistband of his boxers. The way he looks down at me makes my whole body fizzy. I have to glance away, or I'm going to combust right here on his bed.

I slide his boxers and pants down to the floor and he

steps out of them. I reach around and cup his ass cheeks. I've been wanting to do that for weeks now. He's got such an amazing, round ass.

I take him into my mouth and he gives a quiet intake of breath that makes me feel really confident in what I'm doing. But I don't want this to be over too soon, so I let go of him and scoot back on the bed. He hovers over me, stopping for a moment to kiss me on the mouth, and then straddles me, as he undoes the front clasp of my bra. As I gaze at his chest, it's nearly impossible for me to believe that I have him right now. This gorgeous, confident man who so many girls would love to have one night with is on top of me. I can't help a smile.

He furrows his brow, smiling back. "What?" he asks, hand on my bare breast.

"Nothing," I say.

He shuts me up with a kiss on my mouth as he holds himself just above me and then releases his weight down on me, our bare bodies melded together.

I'm not laughing anymore as I run my hands through his hair and lift my hips to feel him against me. We move together, our bodies in rhythm, even though my underwear is still a barrier between us.

He moves down my body, stopping to take my nipple into his mouth, which has me arching my back. He continues on, kissing the insides of my thighs, making me wiggle with want. He slides his finger inside my underwear and I gasp as he touches me.

He looks up at me. "I love how wet you get for me." Heat seeps up my neck and into my cheeks as my secret of just how into him I am is revealed.

He slides my underwear down my legs, and I'm

completely vulnerable to him. He kisses his way back up my inner thigh and then spreads my legs apart. I grip the sheets as his tongue touches me. My body ignites with sensation, and it's all I can do to stay still for him.

I close my eyes, my whole body tensed, sensations flowing like white-water rapids. When he finally sets me free, I let go with a wail that can definitely be heard next door, and I'm embarrassed about how loud I was. I cover my eyes as he climbs on top of me.

"What?" he says with a chuckle.

"Oh, my God. I was so loud."

He moves my hand from my face. "I love it. You can be as loud as you want."

I point at the wall. "These walls are thin, and there's somebody on the other side of that."

"There's nothing to be embarrassed about, Kylie." The way he says my name with that Southern drawl of his makes everything okay.

He hovers over me, and his very hard cock rests on my belly. "Do you have condoms?" I ask.

He responds by rolling off of me and opening his night-stand drawer. He returns, suited up and ready to go. He kisses me, then pulls back and gazes at me like he has some-thing to say, but the words won't come out.

"Are you good?" I ask.

He gives me a lazy smile. "Yeah. I'm good."

He reaches down between us, and with a push, he's inside me. He goes slow, letting me get used to the pressure, and it doesn't take long until it eases. His weight on top of me, our skin on skin makes me feel so close with him, not just physically but emotionally. It's a higher level of intimacy that I never understood before, even when things were good with Joshua.

I'm enjoying the closeness so much that I barely notice Brett's eyes are closed and his expression is almost pained. "Do you think you'll go again?" he asks.

"No. You can let go." He does, collapsing on me, breathing heavily. I rub his back and kiss his neck as his breathing slows.

He lifts up off me. "I hope I didn't leave you behind."

I smile at him. "I'm all good."

He lies on his side, sliding his arm under his pillow.

I match his pose, and he puts his hand on my hip, possessively. "I didn't like being away from you this week," he says.

"Me either." If he only knew.

"I wanted to text you and see how your new job was going."

"It's going well. Everyone's really welcoming. I feel like part of a team rather than someone on the outside of things. It's pretty cool."

"You don't feel chained to a desk? You had your freedom in your former life."

"Very true. But I don't. I feel like I'm finally coming into my own person after way too long."

"What was holding you back?"

I take a minute to compile my thoughts. "Insecurity, I guess. Lack of encouragement from my mom or dad. School was hard for me. I graduated on time, but it was a serious struggle. If I ever complained about school to my mom, she'd tell me to focus on looking for a husband, then I could quit. My dad would just throw money at a tutor or ask if there was someone I could pay to write a paper for me. He just wanted me to graduate so I wouldn't be an embarrass-ment." I meet his gaze to make sure he's still with me. I know how crazy my family sounds.

He takes my hand, running his thumb over it in a soothing motion, giving me the strength to continue.

"I don't know. I traveled for a while right out of college, then I spent the better part of a year with my aunt when she got sick. Even she never worked or had her own career. She wanted those things for me, but it was hard to hear it from her when she hadn't lived that way. To be honest, I was just afraid. I lacked the confidence it takes to start your own career."

"You seem confident to me—determined and strong."

I smile at him. "That's because I'm desperate. I've escaped my old life and I don't want to have to go back."

He plays with my fingers. "I like being a part of your new life."

My body sings with want for him, and I'm worried I'm getting myself in too deep. I recalibrate and refocus the conversation. "What about you? You started a new life about the time I started mine, moving in here."

He inhales a deep breath and then lets it out. "Yep."

"That's a noble thing you did, living at home all those years to take care of your grandma."

He closes his eyes and rubs his temple, rolling onto his back. "I wasn't just taking care of my grandma."

"No?"

"My mom's had it rough, losing her husband and trying to raise me and my brother. It hasn't been an easy life for her."

"I'll bet."

He frowns, seeming to be in deep thought. "She's struggled with addiction a lot of her life."

"What kind of addiction?"

"Opioids, mainly."

I wince. "That is so hard. I haven't had any experience

with that in my own life, but I've seen documentaries. It's so unfair how it affects vulnerable groups of people."

"It's been hard making ends meet over the years, paying for rehabs that we didn't have the money for."

"How is she doing now?"

"She's been sober for nineteen months."

"That's a long time."

He nods. "It is. She's been sober for a longer period of time than this, though. I wanted to stay there with her, but she said my being there was enabling to her. She pretty much kicked me out of the house—told me that if I stayed, I was putting her sobriety in danger."

"Does that scare you?"

"I'm worried for my mother every day of my life. But I feel better about her sobriety now than I have in a long time. She's got my grandma to take care of, so I think that keeps her focused."

I rub my thumb along his hand. "It probably wasn't easy leaving."

"No, it wasn't. But I'll do anything to keep her healthy." I tear up a little, and he looks at me with a smile. "Don't do that."

"Sorry. It's just so sweet to see how much you love her."

"She's the most important thing to me—she and my grandma, and my brother."

I smile, but my heart sinks. "Your family is everything to you. I envy that. My family has all the money anyone could want, but we don't have a fraction of what you guys have."

He pulls my hand to his lips and kisses my knuckles. "I'm sorry."

"You're apologizing to me for being rich. That's kind of messed up."

He just stares at me, threading his fingers through mine.

"I wanted to meet your mom and your grandma the other day," I say.

"That's not how I wanted to introduce you to them."

"I totally understand. It wasn't an appropriate time."

He focuses on my hand. "I would still like to introduce you to them, though."

"I'd love to meet them. And I'd like to spend time with your brother, too."

"I could do without you hanging with him for a while. He's going through a selfish phase."

"How old is he, nineteen?"

"Yeah."

"I think everyone goes through a selfish phase at nineteen."

"Probably. But we can't afford his selfish phase. We need him to help. And we need him to not be irresponsible."

"It's got to be hard for you. You must feel out of control."

"That's a good way to put it."

I kiss him and then pull back. "Thank you for sharing that with me."

"Thanks for listening."

We kiss again, and keep kissing for a long time, until he finally rolls over on top of me. Our bodies move together, his erection growing against my leg. I'm overcome with passion or lust or some feeling I can't put a name to. Whatever it is, I've never felt it before, not even for Joshua after years of being with him.

Brett reaches into the nightstand drawer and pulls out a condom, readying himself. As he pushes inside of me, he moves slowly, taking time to kiss me. The buildup inside of me comes gradually and reaches all the way up through my chest, squeezing my heart. I grasp his shoulders, letting him know it's time for me. We collapse together and he kisses my neck, my cheek, and then my lips, staring at me wordlessly. I can't help but wonder if he's feeling even a fraction of what I am.

25

BRETT

"I can't believe I got you out tonight. You've been MIA," Cohen says.

"Yeah, sorry about that."

"Where is Kylie tonight?"

"Working late."

"Ah. I'll try not to get my feelings hurt knowing I was your second choice. She is way hotter than me."

Logan, on the other side of the bar, grabs a mug and pulls a beer from the tap. "Ah, don't be down on yourself, cuz. You're beautiful to me." He blows Cohen a kiss with a wink.

Cohen eyeballs his cousin as he walks to the other end of the bar to deliver the beer, and then turns to me. "How's it going with her?"

It's a loaded question and one I'm not sure I want to answer. "Good."

"That's not very convincing," he says.

I shift in my seat. "It's just a lot."

"How so?"

"I don't feel very in control."

"Yeah, sounds like love to me."

My chest ignites at the word.

"Sorry, too much?" he asks.

"I think it's all too much. I'm trying to be cool with it, but she's still staying with Jack Massey."

"Oh." The look on Cohen's face indicates I'm not crazy to be worried. He cocks his head to the side, changing his tune. "Nothing's happening between them, though, right?"

"That's the narrative."

"You don't believe her?"

I consider this. "I believe her. I just don't trust him."

"Look, man, I know what went down between him and Tori last year, but Jack's not a bad guy. You know that, right? I really don't think he would do that to you. I think he's more interested in getting back in your good graces."

"Have you been talking to him?"

"No, not really. I mean, he's made a few off-the-cuff remarks here and there over the months. He used to be a part of our group. I think he wishes he could be again."

"That's not happening. Not after what he did to Tori. Nobody in this group would pick him over Tori."

"Except maybe Bailey," Cohen says.

I shrug my agreement.

"Is that the only thing bothering you? Her living with him?" Cohen asks.

"Maybe not. I don't know where it's going. I mean, everything's all roses right now, but I have a feeling she's going to get tired of my schedule really quick. I've got to go to my mom's tomorrow night and spend the night. I'll be there all day on Saturday to watch my grandma. My mom's got a twelve-hour shift that starts at six a.m." I glance over at him. "I've been down this road before, you know."

He nods. "I remember. Madison, right?"

I just look at my beer, the weight of my life bearing down on my shoulders.

"How's your brother been since you moved out?" he asks. "Is he helping like he should?"

"If it's convenient for him. But I can't be too pissed off at him. He's got school and a social life."

"You've got work and a social life."

I shrug. "I'm used to helping more than he is."

"Maybe it's time he gets used to it. Just saying."

Logan appears in front of us. "Another round?" I consider my beer and then check my phone. Logan smirks at me. "Ask her what kind you should get. Tell her I've got a new lager you might like."

"Fuck you," I say. But he's right. When's the last time I checked my phone before wondering if I should have another beer? I am losing control in this relationship. I've got to set some boundaries. I just hope I can stick to them.

26

KYLIE

It's hard for me to believe things are going as well as they are. Last week, I was getting my feet wet, acclimating to the project, which has been to scout out organizations across the southeast who may be willing to sponsor stays for families for the week at cost. Initially, I was to have turned my results over to Jack, and then he would take it from there, but I've convinced him to let me make a presentation explaining my results. My plan to knock their socks off is underway. Now I've just got to figure out how to get them barefooted.

My phone dings, and I see it's a text from Brett.

Are you ready to make your presentation?

As I'll ever be.

You're going to kill it.

I reply with a smiley face, which matches my own expression. Part of the reason I'm not as nervous as I should be is because of Brett. His assurance in me builds my own confidence.

Jack's assistant peeks around the wall of my cubicle. "They're ready for you." I nod and grab my laptop.

When I step into the conference room, my heart pounds as I see Robert sitting there. I had asked Jack who would be in the meeting, and he said just him, Easton from Group Sales, a guy from Accounting, someone from Marketing, and Janelle, who heads PR, which was going to be scary enough as it was. I'm jumping in at the start of a planned budget meeting. I plaster on a smile. "Hi, everyone."

"Kylie, I hope you don't mind if I sit in," Robert says. "I was intrigued when Jack told me you'd requested to make a presentation."

"It's no problem," I say. "I'll talk to anyone who wants to listen."

The room echoes with a courtesy laugh, and I point to the projector. "Do you mind if I hook up?"

"Please," Robert says.

I quickly get set up. I've never given one of these before, so I stayed late last night to figure out how to use the equipment. I grab the remote for the PowerPoint and get us started. "I was given a goal to find contact info for fifty organizations who would be good to solicit for our outreach initiative. Once I hit that goal, I drilled in on each organization to gather more information so that whoever reached out to them would know more about the company, their past philanthropy efforts, the correct contact person who would actually take the call...."

This elicits another laugh, which I wasn't really going for, but okay.

I continue. "In this process, I did what I do best and just started talking to people. And then people would refer me to other people, and then it kind of snowballed. As a result, I have made solid contacts with twenty-two of these resorts, and they're ready to sign on as soon as we can present them a contract."

I continue on with the presentation, showing the various organizations and what they focus on, explaining that I worked with Jack on details, pricing, timelines, etc. At the end, Robert studies me, as my heart spins, waiting for his verdict.

"This is really impressive, Kylie."

I give a contrite nod. "Thank you, sir. I actually enjoyed doing it."

"Would you like to do it some more?"

I shrug. "Sure. I can keep going as long as you'd like me to."

"I mean, would you like a permanent position in Outreach?"

I can't contain my smile. "Yes, I would love one."

Robert turns to Jack. "Jack and I will discuss title, salary, responsibilities, and we'll come back to you with an offer in the next day or two. Will that work?"

"Wonderfully," I say. "Thank you for giving me the opportunity."

"Thank you for taking the ball into the end zone." He opens his laptop. "Let's move on to the budget. I'll sit in on this as well." He glances up at me. "You may go, Kylie."

I grab my stuff and exit the room, grinning like an idiot. Just as I'm getting seated, Bailey pops her head around the corner. "So, how did it go?"

"It went really well," I say, trying to contain my excitement.

"Clearly it did. Look at you. I haven't seen you this happy since you walked in the door."

"I think I might've landed a job—a permanent one."

She holds out her arms. "Congratulations." I stand up and we embrace. She pulls away, smiling at me, but her eyebrows are drawn together. "Can I just say I'm sorry?"

I swallow hard, ready to address the elephant in the room. I was kind of hoping it would just tromp away. "What for? You haven't done anything."

"I did do something pretty horrible. I ghosted you after that night we went out."

I grab her hands. "I totally got it, though. You don't know me. I'm sure I seemed like I was just jumping from one guy to the next. But I swear I wasn't."

"I know you weren't. And even if you were, that's not any of my business."

"It would totally have been your business. You had just told me how you felt about Jack."

She shakes her head. "I'm just such a freaking hot mess. I hope you'll forgive me and we can move forward?"

"Nothing to forgive. I'm just thrilled that we cleared the air."

"I know you're probably seeing Brett tonight, but Simone and I are going out and we'd love to have you join us." She points at me. "But girls only."

"I'd actually love to. Brett is going to his mom's house tonight."

She clasps her hands together. "Perfect. I'll text you the plan."

She heads off, and I pull out my phone to text Brett, but I want to tell him some of my good news in person, so I just text him the part about going out with Bailey and tell him I hope his day is going well. He responds.

That's great. Bailey and Simone are cool. You'll have a good time.

I sit back in my seat, wondering how this day could possibly get any better.

27

BRETT

I lean against my truck, waiting for Kylie to come out of her office. I just want to see her face before I head to my mom's house.

I haven't seen her much at all this week. She's been working a lot of late nights. I tell myself it's not my insecurity, but part of me wants her to see me more than anything. She texted a while ago to say she's having a girls' night with Bailey and Simone. I'm happy that she's cool with Bailey again, but the three of them are bound to turn heads tonight. I want to kiss her and give her something to think about before she heads out for the night.

A group of corporate drones come out together—Easton, Taylor, some asshole I don't recognize, Janelle, Bailey, Kylie, and of course, Jack Massey. They're all smiling and laughing, Kylie beaming from ear to ear. "Hey," she says with wide eyes as she spots me.

"What's up?" I ask.

"Your girl," Bailey says, beaming at her.

Kylie's face goes red, and the rest of them look like they're proud of themselves or something.

Bailey squeezes Kylie's shoulders. "She's the newest official member of Corporate."

"You got a permanent job?" I ask.

"Yeah," she says. "I guess the presentation went okay."

I make eye contact with Jack, who stares back at me with his hands in his pockets. I don't know if I want to thank him or punch him in the face.

"That's awesome," I say, giving her a hug.

"Thank you. I don't even know what to say." She glances around at the group. "You're all so wonderful. I can't believe I'm gonna be your new co-worker permanently."

"You deserve it," Easton says. "You kicked ass these past two weeks."

I study him. Is this another asshole I need to worry about?

"Are you coming to eat with us?" Janelle asks me.

I look at Kylie, confused, and she says, "We're going to happy hour. Can you come?"

"I've got to go to my mom's," I say, hoping to hell she remembered that.

She shakes her head. "Of course. I knew that. I just didn't know when you had to leave."

"Can you come for one drink?" Bailey asks.

I look at this group of people and Jack standing there so smug, like he's responsible for the earth spinning. I glance down at my phone to check the time. I have maybe enough for one beer if I drink it through a straw.

Kylie turns to Jack and they're discussing something, huddled together. I freaking hate that she lives with him and they have this strong connection. She sees him way more than she sees me. For all I know, they're sleeping in the same bed. I know that's ridiculous when she's told me repeatedly to trust her, but it's hard, especially when I see how close they've gotten both at work and personally.

"Let me check," I say and step away from the group, calling Matthew. He picks up the phone with an irritated, "What?"

"Are you going out tonight?"

"Later," he says.

"What time?"

"I don't know."

"Can you stay with Mimi for a couple of hours?"

"I thought you were coming right after work?"

"I've got something to do for an hour or two. Can you at least stay there till nine?"

He gives an irritated sigh. "I guess, but I'm leaving here at nine."

"That's fine. Thanks."

"Whatever." He hangs up and I pocket my phone, rejoining the group. "I can come for a drink."

"Oh, good," Kylie says, wrapping her arms around me, and I hold on to her, feeling less in control than ever.

WE GO to an Italian restaurant off property and get a table. This is more than drinks. This is dinner with expensive bottles of wine that Bailey ordered with advice from Kylie. A real cloth-napkin-in-your-lap kind of joint. I've been to these sorts of restaurants with Robert, but never when I was growing up. We were lucky to get a bag of fast food back then. I'll never get used to this kind of life. But it's clear that Kylie's very comfortable at a place like this.

She turns to me and squeezes my knee. "I hope this is okay? I know you were only expecting to get a drink."

"It's fine. I just want to see you for a minute."

She smiles at me and then kisses me. When she focuses on her menu, I look across the table at Jack, who catches my eye and then inspects his own menu. I hate how it eats at me that he's in her life the way he is.

She lays down her menu. "Do you know what you want to eat?"

"I really don't care. You can order for me if you want."

"Really? What if I order something you don't like?"

"I'm not picky. I like trying new things," I say, hoping this impresses her, my nonchalance about being here, my coolness with all of this—her, Jack, this stupid restaurant.

"So what are you gonna do with your grandma tomorrow?" she asks.

I know she's just being kind and making conversation, but she really doesn't understand that there's nothing to be done with my grandma other than to sit there with her, watching the Food Network, waiting for her to stand up and walk around the place looking for something that doesn't exist. All I can do is follow along beside her in case she stumbles, get her to the bathroom, and change her diaper. I don't think this is what Kylie wants to hear right now or at any time.

"I'm not sure," I say. "Just spending time with her."

She smiles that adoring smile that makes me feel like the only man on earth she could ever want, and I know I'm in way over my head.

After we eat and everyone takes a bite of a couple of desserts, I check my phone. "I've got to get going," I say loudly enough to get everyone's attention. I hold up my phone. "Who do I Venmo for Kylie and me?"

"I've got the bill," Jack says.

I nod at Kylie, keeping my eyes on Jack. "I'll pay for ours."

"I'm putting it on my corporate card."

"I don't fucking care," I say.

"Brett," Kylie says under her breath.

I take a beat and then pocket my phone. "Fine." I slide my chair back and Kylie gets up with me.

"I'll walk you out," she says, and then we head toward the door, everyone giving me their goodbyes.

We stand by my truck, and she moves her hands up my arms and across my shoulders. "Thank you so much for coming out. I was so glad to get to see you even for a couple of hours. I've missed you so much this week."

I put my hands on her waist. "I've missed you, too. What are you doing tomorrow night?"

"Whatever you want."

I move my hands up her torso. "I don't know if I'll ever want to leave the bed."

"That's absolutely fine with me."

I kiss her, and she moves her hand across my neck, threading her fingers in my hair as we kiss like we've been separated for a year. She pulls away, panting, "I wish we could go somewhere."

I clench my eyes shut, wishing we wouldn't have stayed at that stupid restaurant so long.

She presses herself against me. "How much time do you have?"

It's more than I can resist. "Get in the car," I say, and she hustles around to the other side, I drive to my place and whisk her inside. Val and Cohen are hanging out on the couch with Tori in the side chair.

I stand there running my hands through my hair,

wanting them to magically get up and leave. "You okay?" Val asks.

"Yeah," I say, glancing around. Tori gives me a funny look and then smiles. "Let's head over to my place," she says to the guys, and then everyone seems to catch on.

"Cool," Cohen says, giving me a grin as the three of them head out.

As soon as the door shuts, Kylie and I are all over each other. I rid her of her blouse and bra, and she pulls my shirt over my head. We can't stop kissing, hands all over one another. I unzip her pants and let them fall to the ground, sliding her underwear down. She steps out of them and I hike her up onto the dining room table. I fall to my knees and spread her thighs, pulling her to the edge.

She lets out a moan as I close in on her, wrapping her legs around my neck, leaning back on the palms of her hands.

I stand up, pulling a condom out of my pocket before dropping my shorts to the floor. I ready myself and then push into her. The emotions inside of me are almost more than I can handle as I drive into her, wanting to make her mine, and not just for tonight.

She wraps her legs around my back and grips my shoulders as I pick her up and press her against the wall. She lets out a wail, and I know it's time to let go inside of her, as much as I want this moment to last all night.

As we come down from the high of lust for one another, she kisses me and I kiss back, not wanting to stop. "I'm crazy about you," she whispers into my ear, and I close my eyes, drinking in her words, wanting to go a step further and tell her how I really feel in three words.

Instead, I kiss her some more and then pull away from her. "I've got to get going."

She nods. "I know. I'm sorry if I've made you late."

"It'll be fine. I'll text Matthew before I head out."

We both get dressed and she checks her phone. "They're heading to the Circle. I can walk."

"I'll drop you down there."

"Okay," she says, giving me another kiss. "I'll miss you tonight."

"I'll miss you, too." She has no idea how much I mean it.

28

BRETT

As I pull into the entrance of our trailer park, I'm struck by the way my life has veered paths from how I grew up. There shouldn't be any shame in eating at a fancy Italian restaurant, but still, being back here makes me feel like a fraud.

I pull up to my mom's trailer, and an ache forms in the pit of my gut as I don't see my brother's car. I jump out of the truck and head to the door, which is ajar. I open it and am met with panic when I don't find my grandmother in her recliner.

"Mimi?" I say. I go to the bathroom, and it's empty. "Mimi," I shout, getting louder, but our trailer only has two bedrooms, and I've searched them both in seconds. I call my brother, but he doesn't pick up. I text him.

Where are you? Where is Mimi? Do you have her?

No response. I text again.

Did you guys go to the store or something?

It's wishful thinking, but I'm desperate. I run outside, looking all around. "Mimi?" I call out. I start banging on doors. I go to Mr. Cotton's door first. "Mr. Cotton? Have you seen my grandmother?"

"No," he shouts from inside and then says something about me needing to keep a better eye on her.

I bang on another door. "George, have you seen my grandmother?"

His wife comes to the door. "Did you lose her again?"

"I'm not sure. Matthew's not answering his phone." I pull out my phone and call him again. "Have you seen him?" I ask, listening to the phone ring on the other end.

"Honey, I don't pay attention to what's going on outside this door. I've got my show on."

I walk away, scouring the place, but she's nowhere to be found.

I remember where she went last time and head that way, toward the street. Two people huddle over something on the side of the road, and I run toward them. My heart thunders the closer I get, and I hope against all hope that it's not my grandma.

"What's happening?" I shout.

"She was hit by a car."

My hand flies to my mouth as the pasta I just ate threatens to make its way back up. I move in closer, but I don't need to look at her face, because those are her house shoes.

The man is saying something about the police, as the woman shouts about CPR.

I spring into action. "Move," I yell.

They scatter out of my way, and I start the steps. They come back to me like riding a bike. I look at the man. "Call 911."

I start compressions.

29

KYLIE

It's really strange that I haven't heard from Brett all day. I texted him last night when I got home with a funny note about our quickie and a flame emoji, but he never responded. I keep checking my phone, but there's been nothing from him.

It's hard for me to imagine he's mad at me. We didn't have any kind of fight or anything—much the opposite. We had the hottest sex of my life. Of course, the bar was low thanks to Joshua. But still.

"You should just go over there," Jack says from his spot on the couch.

I sit at the dining room table, tapping my foot. "That seems kind of desperate."

"Weren't you supposed to have plans with him tonight?"

"Yeah. You don't think I should be worried about him, do you?"

He shrugs. "I don't know, to be honest with you. Like I've mentioned, he's broken a lot of hearts around here. But as possessive as he has been of you, it's kind of hard for me to believe he would blow you off. Do you want me to text him?"

"No. But thank you."

"I could text him something about Robert—a work question, just to see if he responds. That way you know his phone isn't in the Gulf of Mexico or anything."

I consider this. "You could text him and ask him if he's going to be using the boat tonight." He gets his phone, and I clench my eyes shut. "No, don't do that. I don't wanna play that game." Jack sets his phone down and picks up his tablet.

"I'm going over there," I say.

"Good decision. If he's blowing you off, then fuck him. Come back here and we'll watch some depressing movie and you can drown your sorrows in a bottle of wine."

I force a smile. "Let's hope it doesn't come to that."

I drive over to Brett's street and park in front of his unit. As I walk up the steps, my heart gains a few pounds. The door is cracked open, and there're voices inside.

I push it open and find Bailey, Simone, Cohen, Logan, Isaac, and Val standing around the living room, talking in hushed tones. "What's going on?" I ask as the blood drains out of my face.

"Hey," Bailey says. "I was just getting ready to text you."

"What is it?" I say, my voice becoming shrill.

She puts a finger over her lips and ushers me outside. "Brett's grandmother was killed last night in a hit-and-run."

I have to steady myself. "Oh, my God. When? What happened?"

"I'm piecing things together from what Tori has told Logan, but it sounds like nobody was home when he got there last night. I think his little brother was supposed to be watching her. I'm not really sure."

I swallow hard. "So when you say hit by a car, do you mean while she was in another car, or was she..." I can't even bring myself to say the words.

"No, she wandered out to the street, apparently."

I bite on my thumbnail, thinking about what Brett and I were doing right before he left, and it hits me like a ton of bricks falling from the sky that I held him up from getting there on time.

"You don't look good," Bailey says. "I think you should sit down."

"I need to go see him. Where is he?"

"Tori is with him in his room. He doesn't want to see anyone."

"Yeah, but this is me. I need to see him."

Bailey looks pained. She pulls out her phone and shows me a text. It's from Tori.

If Kylie shows up, please don't send her back here. Brett says he doesn't want to see her right now.

I feel like someone just stuck a sword in my gut.

Bailey rubs my shoulder. "I'm so sorry, sweetie. I really am."

I meet Bailey's frown, and I say, "Do you think there's any chance she's lying?"

She exhales a deep breath. "I really don't think so. She's just not like that. She's as straightforward as they come, and she's not manipulative. And..."

"And what?"

"And someone asked about you earlier and I heard him say he didn't want to see you right now."

My heart plummets. "Is that what he said? Is that exactly how he said it?"

"I think his exact words were, *I just can't.*"

I collapse into a plastic chair on the front porch.

Bailey peers inside. "Tori's out. Let's hear what she has to say."

Bailey walks into the house, leaving the door half-open for me. I stand up and listen in.

"You guys are great for being here for him," Tori says, "and he really appreciates you all. He's just here to shower and get back to his mom. He even wants me to leave."

There's a low mumble from the room, and then people start filing out. Everyone disperses toward their homes, while Tori closes the door behind her.

She looks up at me, her eyes going wide at the sight of me for a second, and then she gives a partial smile and walks toward her unit.

I rub my temple as I pad toward my car, my head spinning.

30

BRETT

We decided on a graveside service to keep things small, but even so, there's way more people here than I expected—my mom's AA group, a ton of her co-workers, some of my grandmother's old friends who we haven't seen much of since she got sick, and a handful of our neighbors.

The preacher drones on about life and death, quoting scripture and saying things about my grandmother that could apply to anyone in attendance today. Seventy-six years of a full and important life reduced to this atrocity. What a disservice.

After the ceremony, we turn around and are bombarded by people wanting to speak to us. They form a line, and we greet them one at a time. I feel like a broken record telling people thank you and that, yes, she was an incredible woman. But what I want to say to most of these people is, *Where the fuck have you been for the past three years that she was so sick?*

Matthew is worthless right now. He can't look anyone in the eye, and I can tell this is excruciating for him. I reach around Tori, who stands between us, and tap him on the arm. "Go sit in the car." He bolts without hesitation.

Robert and Catherine are next in line. They both give me a hug and their condolences. "Take as much time as you need," Robert says. "And let me know what I can do. I feel helpless."

Join the club.

I greet another few people, and then my friends are next in line. I'm overwhelmed with gratitude for them. They all hug me, and the girls give me kisses on the cheek, all telling me how sorry they are and how much they love me. As much as I love each of them, I can't help looking past them to see if Kylie's here. But I don't find her.

"We'll be gathered at our place this evening if you'd like to come over when you get home," Simone says.

"You all don't have to wait around for me. I don't even know what I'm doing right now."

"We just want to be available if you need us," Bailey says.

I nod, trying to keep it together. After they clear out, I'm met face-to-face with Jack Massey. It's all I can do to keep from rolling my eyes. "I'm so sorry," he says.

I just nod, holding my mouth in a tight line so I don't say something to embarrass my family.

"She was a beautiful woman. I only met her that once, but I could tell you got your dry sense of humor from her."

I'm confused at first, and then I rewind back to when he first came to work at the resort. He and I were just getting to know each other. There was tension because we were both Robert's boys, and he was the new one. I invited him for Sunday dinner at my mom's house just to watch him squirm, rich boy that he is. But he couldn't have been more gracious. He fit in with my family better than I do sometimes, son of a bitch.

I'm unable to open my mouth as the dam presses behind my eyes, threatening to break at any moment.

He gives me sort of a half wave and then steps off.

I look down the rest of the line and don't find Kylie anywhere. I haven't been able to bring myself to text her since it happened. I don't know if I can look her in the eye. What happened is my fault and my fault alone. I will bear that burden for the rest of my life. The reason I can't connect with her is because I know I can't have her anymore. Still, part of me just needs to know if she came.

My feet move before my brain does. "Jack," I call out, and he turns around. I walk over to him, but when I reach him, I'm unable to bring words to my lips.

"Kylie?" he asks.

I hesitate and then just nod.

He points to the road. "She's in the car. Do you want me to send her over here?"

I shake my head. "No. Thanks."

I walk over to continue my duty of greeting people, my gut twisting like a pretzel.

31

KYLIE

I'm wrapping up my last email for the day when Bailey peeks around the wall of my cubicle. "Thanks for your help today with Family Day."

I twirl around to face her and force a smile, not sure when I'll ever be able to do that naturally again. "Sure. I enjoyed it."

"Your party planning skills are really coming in handy. I can't believe you never got paid for that before."

"Trust me, I was compensated."

"Are you bringing anybody in from Oklahoma for it?" Bailey asks.

My stomachs sours, matching the ongoing fog I've had over my head for weeks. "No, not really anyone to invite."

She frowns. "I know you and your dad aren't on the best of terms right now. What about your mom?"

"My mom lives in California. Something called Family Day wouldn't really be her thing."

"Understood."

I just want to get back to work and my depression, but I

remind myself that conversations need to go both ways. "What about you? What's your family like?"

She gives me a wry smile. "Oh, you don't wanna crawl down that deep, dark hole."

I lift an eyebrow. "I think I might."

"My mom and all her siblings went in together on a lottery ticket that hit big, and now they own and run a casino where we're from in Biloxi, Mississippi."

"That sounds amazing."

"Redneck as hell. I have twenty-seven cousins and most all of them work there. I'm the black sheep because I'm here, and none of them let me forget it for a second."

"Sounds like they just want you there with them."

She shrugs. "I guess, so they can meddle...especially in my love life. They're always getting married and want the same for me. I can't take another wedding. You wouldn't believe how many I've been to just this year. My closet is full of ugly bridesmaid dresses."

I fumble with a pen on my desk. "That actually sounds really nice."

She gives me a smile, but I can tell her heart isn't totally in it.

"Is everything okay?" I ask.

"It's fine." She winces. "I just really wish I could invite you out with us tonight."

My heart stings. "It's totally fine. It's more important for you to take care of Brett right now."

"I know, but you're important, too."

Bailey has been great about getting me out of the office for lunch a couple of times a week this past month since Brett's grandma died, and I really appreciate her efforts. But her allegiance is to Brett, and I understand a hundred percent. I'm the new girl, and they've known him for years. And besides, he needs them more than I do right now.

"Maybe we'll plan a girls' night," Bailey says.

My gut wrenches as I remember what happened the last time we had planned a girls' night.

I know none of the women in the group want to be seen as siding with me. And I hate more than anything that there are sides. I just want to be with him, but I also want to respect what he's going through and remember my fault in it.

Bailey squeezes my shoulder and then steps away. My text alert dings, and I check my phone. I let out a sigh when I see Joshua's name.

I'm in town to see you. Can you spare a few minutes for me?

I drop the phone in my lap, closing my eyes.

"Boy." I look up to see Jack standing there. "That looks serious. You okay?"

"I'm fine. It's just my ex. He's here in town."

"I'm guessing he wants to meet with you."

"I'm just so exhausted these days. I don't think I have the fight to say no."

"I was coming over here to tell you that Easton and I are going to grab something to eat after work at the Circle. If you want, you can meet him down there and we'll be around if you need backup."

I look up at Jack and all his good-guy glory. "I don't know what I would've done this past month without you."

"I wish I could say I've done something. Honestly, it feels good to have a friend again."

"Easton's your friend."

"Yeah, but he's also an idiot." He smiles, revealing his lie.

"That doesn't sound like a bad idea, actually—not that I

think he's going to do anything nefarious, but I may need a drink after dealing with him."

"Sounds good. We're about to head out if you want to wrap up."

"Okay."

IT GIVES me no small sense of joy to walk up to the entrance of the Circle flanked by Jack and Easton, two big, good-looking guys. Joshua shuffles his feet, crossing his arms over his chest and then putting his hands on his hips, clearly rattled. Good.

We all walk up to him, frowns all around. "Are you okay, Kylie?" Jack asks.

"I'm okay," I say.

"We'll be right around the corner when you're done."

"Or if you need us," Easton tosses in.

"I'm her ex, not a rapist," Joshua says.

"We'll see about that," Jack says, and he and Easton head off.

"You brought in the cavalry to see me?" Joshua asks.

I point to a bench. "Let's just get this over with."

He sits down, glancing around. "You've done okay for yourself. This place is pretty nice."

"I think so."

"But our house is a lot nicer."

"*We* don't have a house. You have a house."

"It was getting ready to be your house, too."

"Yeah, I wonder what happened there?"

"Look, I know I fucked up royally. I just got caught up in the secret of it all. I really didn't mean to hurt you."

"Out of curiosity, were you going to continue that affair well into our marriage?"

"I swear, I told her it had to end on our wedding day. You can ask her."

"No, thanks." I consider him. "How's that going, anyway? I've been following some of the group's Instagrams, and I don't see her in their posts."

He shuffles in his seat. "It's over. Bryce kicked her out after you exposed us. She didn't want to move in with her mom and dad, so I let her stay at the house until she could get something figured out. I guess in her mind, we were going to be together."

"You suddenly didn't want her anymore?"

"Not for a wife. It was only about the sex."

My stomach rolls.

"Sorry," he says.

I wave him off. "If it was about the sex with her, what was it about with me?"

"You're exactly the kind of girl I always wanted to marry. You're sweet and kind and loving. You're devoted and dedicated and you love taking care of people. I really couldn't have asked for anything more."

"Then why did you have to mess it up?"

He shakes his head. "Because I'm an idiot. I think I just had a fucked-up perception of marriage. I was talking to my dad about it once, how I didn't know if I was ready to be with one woman for the rest of my life. He winked at me and told me it didn't have to be that way. He gave me this kind of fucked-up advice about treating your wife like a queen and keeping her happy and then having a little tail on the side."

I wince. "Tail? Really?"

"I know. But I thought it was a way that I could move

forward with marriage. When your aunt made you promise to wait until you were twenty-five, it was like a godsend. You notice I never really argued that much."

I think about it. "No, you didn't."

"I thought, *Thank God. Because I'm not ready*. And then the closer it came to time, the more I acted out, I guess. I don't know."

I process what he's saying, and in a weird way, I get it. "Thank you for telling me all this. It helps me understand."

"You don't need to thank me for anything ever again. So what's going on with you here? What's your job?"

A sense of pride boils up inside of me. "I'm the outreach coordinator."

"What's that?"

"I work to get grants for families to come stay at the resort free of cost." I explain a little about the resort's specializations.

"Wow. That sounds...it actually sounds perfect for you."

"Really?"

"Yeah, it does. You're tenacious. You go for what you want. You're personable, and you care about people."

I allow myself a moment of pride, though I've felt nothing but shame the past month.

"Did your dad ever break down and send you any money?" he asks.

"Not a dime. But to be fair, Samantha gave me some to get down here."

"God, that makes me feel like shit. I wish you would've let me give you some."

I shrug. "It turns out I didn't need it."

He smiles at me. "Sounds like you're thriving here."

I look away, feeling terrible for thriving, even just at work, when Brett is in so much pain.

"Are you dating one of those guys who wanted to kick my ass?"

"No," I say, picking at my fingernail.

"Ah, but you are dating someone? I should've known."

"No, I'm definitely not...not anymore."

"What happened?"

I shake my head. "I don't wanna talk about it."

He lowers his chin, giving me that look, and I know exactly what's coming next. "So if you're single, want to go knock one out for old time's sake?"

I glare at him. "No, I do not."

He smiles. "I had to check."

"What are you doing here, anyway?" I ask.

"The goal was to get you to come home. But to be honest, I don't think I'm ready to be in a relationship right now."

"Uh, ya think?"

He gives a contrite smile, looking down at his lap.

"When you say the goal was to get me to come home, whose goal was it?" I ask.

He cuts his gaze at me. "You know whose goal it was."

I exhale a deep breath. "My dad has not said boo to me in weeks. And now he sends you down here to do his dirty work."

"Your dad's an extremely proud man. He likes everyone in his orbit to be under his thumb."

I squint into the distance. "I lived the life of his good little girl for twenty-five years."

"And now you're living your own life. How does that feel?"

The bittersweet ache in my chest grasps me, because as long as Brett is hurting, I'll never feel okay.

"Are you hungry?" Joshua asks.

"Not really."

"Let me rephrase that. I'm hungry. Do you want to come sit with me while I eat and tell me about what's happening with this new guy of yours?"

I stand up. "I'll go sit with you. Let me introduce you to the Circle."

"If the Circle's got a fried seafood platter, then I'm in."

"I'm sure we can rustle one up."

32

BRETT

Tori puts her napkin on the table. "That was so good, Melody. It's been way too long since I've had your lasagna."

"That's for sure," my mom says. "It's good seeing you. I've missed having you around."

Tori nods, looking down at her lap. We all know that she doesn't come around because she doesn't want to run into her own mother two doors down. But she's risked it to be with me these past six weeks for Sunday dinner.

"I've got some news for you boys," my mom says. Matthew looks up from his plate with a frown.

"I'm selling the trailer."

"Wait, what?" Matthew asks. "Why?"

"The only reason we stayed here all these years was because it was familiar to Mimi. I didn't want to move her to a new place and add more stress to her situation. But I'm doing better, and I'm a supervisor now at the hospital. Lead patient care coordinator. I got a salary increase."

"Why didn't you tell me?" I ask.

She shrugs. "It didn't seem real. I just wanted to wait

until I got my first paycheck with the new salary, I guess." She smiles.

It's just like my mom to bury the lead. I don't want to make too big of a deal out of this promotion, because I'm not sure this is her dream. She tried going to school to be a nurse, but life, and her addiction, always got in the way. But maybe someday she can still make that happen.

"That's fantastic," Tori says.

"Thanks."

"Where am I going to live?" Matthew asks.

"You can come with me, hon. Or you can stay at the dorm next year if you want. It's time for us all to move on."

A silence falls over us. I knew this time would come, and I even thought it might be liberating in some sick way, but I can't get past the way it happened—the pain my grandma must have experienced. I've just wanted to be here since it happened, as if my presence could change the outcome of that night.

"I've appreciated you being here and helping with everything," my mom says, "but I need my space as much as you need yours."

I try not to let her words sting. "Okay. When are you moving?"

"I've got a real estate agent who's going to help me sell this trailer. His name is Scott Wills." She pauses, giving a significant smile. Tori and I glance at one another. "I won't get much for it, of course, but it is paid off, so it will be a little...enough for a small down payment for the condo I'm looking at."

"Is it in Wabash?" Matthew asks.

"Nope. Panama City."

Tori and I lift our eyebrows at one another.

"Is it on the beach?" he asks.

"I'm not the hospital administrator," my mom says with a smile. "It's off Highway 98."

"That sounds wonderful, Melody," Tori says.

"It does, Mom," I say. "Let me know when this will all go down. Matthew and I will get you moved."

"Thanks, hon. I'll keep you posted."

As we finish cleaning up the dishes, my mom says, "I think I'm gonna go to bed early if y'all don't mind."

Tori and I both give our hugs and goodbyes and then head out.

Once we're on the highway, Tori says, "Your mom seems to be doing well, considering."

"She's being strong for me and Matthew. She knows how guilty we both feel."

"Possibly. But even so, she's doing okay. Did you see the look in her eye when she said the name of that real estate agent?"

I roll my eyes. "I saw it."

"He might be a decent guy."

"If history repeats..."

"She's different now. She's better. It's pretty clear. I've had a bird's-eye view all these Sundays we've been over here since the funeral. I've felt okay about leaving these past few weeks, especially if she's got someone to occupy her time."

"I can't think about that. It'll just give me something else to worry about."

"Well, maybe you don't need to worry so much."

I eye her. "Do you know something about this guy?"

"He was a patient at the hospital. She checked his blood pressure and the rest is history."

"How do you know that?"

"Do you think your mom and I only talk when you're around?"

I shift in my seat, feeling left out, but also grateful that my mom has a woman to talk to.

"He's got a clean record. No arrests," she says.

"How in the hell did you find that out?"

"Will you give me some credit? I grew up reading the A to Z Mysteries."

I think about the trail of losers who have come in and out of her life over the years. "I guess that's as good of a start as she's ever had. He's not in AA, is he?"

"And it'd be a problem if he was?"

I take it all in.

"You know, it sounds stupid and cliché, but love heals a lot of wounds." I can tell by the look she's giving me that she's not talking about my mom anymore. I turn the radio up and we ride in silence the rest of the way home.

33

BRETT

Tori and I walk to Family Day at the Circle together. I know Robert has good intentions with this day, but it can't be easy on Tori. Her dad is a piece of shit, and she hasn't spoken to her mom in years. I texted her little brother to see if he was coming, but he just made up a flimsy excuse.

I try to understand things from his perspective, but it's tough. He left home when he was fourteen and moved in with his girlfriend's family, where he's lived ever since. He's not looked back, even to check on Tori. I don't care if she's seven years older. She needs checking on. I guess he thinks that's what I'm here for.

"Looks like we're fashionably late," Tori says as we approach the swarm of people at the pavilion. I text my mom to see if she and Matthew are here yet, and she texts back.

Parking.

An unease bubbles in my stomach as I pocket my phone. "You okay?" Tori asks.

"Of course I'm okay. Why would I not be?"

"Just keep an open mind, okay?"

My mom is bringing her boyfriend. I'm happy for her if she's happy. I just want to make sure he's not an asshole. But I don't tell Tori that's not what's bugging me.

I scour the lawn, looking for Kylie. It's been eight weeks since I've seen her. I know she'll be here, and I just want to put my eyes on her so that I'm not taken off guard, but I can't find her anywhere.

"She's working the family photo booth," Tori says.

I look down at her. "What are you talking about?"

"Kylie. Isn't that who you're looking for?"

I shuffle my feet. "No, I was not looking for her."

Tori just gives me that stupid smile like she knows everything on the damn earth.

"How do you know that, anyway?" I ask.

"She helped plan this whole event with Janelle and Bailey."

I think about Kylie telling me how she planned parties at her dad's company. "Mmm," I utter, keeping my mouth shut.

"She moved out of Jack's place a couple of weeks ago," Tori says.

I shrug like I don't care, but I can't help the wash of relief that floods over me. Besides that, I find myself truly happy for her.

"There's your mom," Tori says.

My mom and Matthew walk our way with a man who looks about a decade older than my mom.

"Hey, honey," my mom says, giving me a hug.

"Hey," I say, pulling away from her and eyeballing the guy.

He holds his hand out to me. "Scott Wills."

"Brett," I say.

"It's certainly nice to meet you," he says with a smile that seems sincere, but we'll see.

I look at Matthew. "What's up?"

Matthew just shrugs, glancing around. I don't know why my mom made him come. He hates being around people like this. I know she's trying to be supportive of me, but I don't like that it means punishing Matthew in the process.

We make small talk about what Scott Mills does and what I do and what this resort is about and blah blah blah. At least he doesn't seem like an asshole.

"Matthew!" I turn around and find Robert beaming from ear to ear as he comes toward my brother. "How in the hell are you?" he asks as he grabs my brother's hand and shakes it, grasping his shoulder.

Matthew beams back at him. When Robert lets go of his hand, Matthew starts wringing them together and rocking from foot to foot, something he does when he's excited.

Robert is one of the few people on earth who's not in Matthew's daily life that Matthew is actually comfortable around. Robert's brother has autism and is the whole reason this resort exists the way it does. I think Matthew gravitates toward Robert because he knows how to talk to him like a typical human and is completely unfazed by awkwardness. Even though Matthew has never been diagnosed with autism, his mannerisms and behaviors can give that appearance.

My mom introduces Scott, and Robert greets him in kind, then turns back to Matthew. They get wrapped up in their own private conversation. Tori has taken an interest in Scott and is quizzing him similarly to a detective with a witness.

My mom smiles at me, pulling me aside. "How are you doing?"

"I'm doing fine."

"I hope so. I think about you all the time, sweetie." She rubs my back. "I just want you to be happy. If I could have that for you and Matthew, I wouldn't need anything else."

I glance at her new guy and then back at her. "You seem happy."

"He's a good guy. I know it's hard to believe that coming from me, but it's different this time."

"Does he drink?"

"He did before he met me, but he stopped, not because he has to but because he says he doesn't really care about it one way or the other. He's really supportive."

"How much older is he?"

She purses her lips at me. "Does that really matter?"

"I'm just curious."

"He's nine years older."

"That doesn't bother you?"

"I think he's handsome. Don't you?"

I look at him, considering. "I guess he's not grotesque."

"Seriously, I'm attracted to him. It's not like he's old enough to be my father or anything."

We stand in silence a moment, glancing around at the people congregating, some at an arts and craft station, some at a corn hole toss, and some filling their plates with barbecue.

"Am I going to get to meet this famous Kylie today?"

I frown at her and then let out a sigh. "How often do you and Tori talk, anyway?"

"I don't know much about her at all, just that things were going really well with the two of you until the night Mimi died?" She looks at me with a question in her eye.

Pain shoots through my chest. "I don't wanna talk about it."

"Well, I do want to talk about it. What happened that night was a horrible tragedy. But it was also an accident. Nobody meant for Mimi to wander out of the house. It just happened."

"It wouldn't have happened if I would've been there."

"It's in the past. You can't punish yourself for the rest of your life. How do you think that makes your brother feel?"

I meet her gaze. "How does how I feel have anything to do with what he feels?"

"Because the more you huff and puff around and punish yourself, the more he does the same. This has killed him. He's failing school."

"He is?" I say, my chest constricting.

"He's already dropped out of his summer class, and now he's threatening not to go back for the fall semester. He left the trailer that night because she was asleep and you were on your way. I've done that before, Brett. I've left her to run out for quick errands. I've left her to go meet my drug dealer."

I wince as a vise grip takes hold of my body.

"Matthew didn't do anything that he didn't learn from me. Until the three of us can forgive ourselves for our sins, none of us will be able to move forward. I need you to forgive yourself."

My mom puts on a smile, looking over my shoulder, and I turn to find Matthew and Robert rejoining us. "Will your brother be here today?" my mom asks. "It's Ethan, right?"

"That's right," Robert says. "He's on his way. I told him I would come get him, but he said he wanted to bring his own car. He said when I pick him up, he's stuck here all day."

We all laugh.

"I know how he feels," Matthew says with a smile.

We all laugh again, and Matthew meets my gaze and

then looks away, the smile leaving his face. My heart breaks to think I'm punishing him without even meaning to. This whole time, I have felt like I was shouldering the blame and the burden so that he wouldn't, but I see now I've just made him feel worse.

I nudge him on the shoulder. "Do you want to go check out those old-school arcade games with me?"

"I'm good," Matthew says, looking away.

"Come with me," I say, and he minds me like he always has. When we get to the arcade, I point at a table. "Sit with me a second."

"We're not gonna play games?"

"In a minute. You know I don't blame you for what happened that night, don't you?"

He just looks all around the place, fidgeting.

"Hey," I say, and he meets my gaze. "That was not your fault. We've all left her there alone at times. She was asleep. You had every right to believe I was coming in minutes. I would've done the same thing if I were you," I say, even though I don't think it's true, at least not since that day we lost her.

"No, you wouldn't have. You would've stayed there with her."

"I left her once," I say.

"When?"

"About three or four months ago. I was over there with her alone, and I wanted a Coke. I went to the convenience store, got a Coke, and came back. She was sitting in the same damn position she was when I left. There's no difference between what I did that day and what you did that night."

He swallows hard, looking down at his hands.

"It's not your fault. Do you hear me?"

He nods.

"How about we both stop beating ourselves up over it? Why don't we both forgive ourselves?"

He nods, but the way his face is scrunched up, I'm afraid he's getting ready to cry.

"What's Centipede? Have you ever played that?"

He looks up, suddenly interested in me. "A couple of times."

"Can you show me how?"

"You hate video games."

"I don't hate them. I just don't know them. I didn't grow up with them like you did."

"I guess I can show you," he says.

"Are you going to get all butt hurt when I kick your ass?"

He gives me half a smile. "As long as you don't act like a bitch when you lose."

My heart warms a few degrees as I follow him through the arcade.

34

KYLIE

Today is definitely the second worst day I've had since I've been here. After two months, I should be over Brett. What's the rule? One month grieving for every two months in a relationship? By those rules, I should've been over this weeks ago.

I'm making progress. I went out last weekend with Taylor, who also works in the business office. And Easton and I have been talking more. We had lunch together earlier this week, and he paid. I wasn't sure if that was just a nice gesture on his part or if it was a date. Either way, when a guy walked in sporting a resort-issued polo and khakis like the ones I've seen Brett wear to work, my heart leapt up into my throat until I figured out it wasn't him.

I guess I've got to give myself a break. This is the first time I've seen him since that awful night. I tried to keep from looking, but I spotted him with Tori, his mom, his little brother, and some man hanging out by the ring toss a while ago, and I've been completely flustered since—not that I didn't start the day a wreck as it was.

Another family steps up, and I smile, directing them to

the backdrop. I snap their picture and ask them to put their email address or phone number into the tablet so that I can send them their pictures. I was thrilled to be able to do this job since I have no family here. But this whole day has made me see just how alone in this world I really am.

I don't have to be alone. I can be in my mom's life, where I feel like a phony, and I can be in my dad's life, where I feel like a child. But even in this life, where I pretty much only have one loyal friend, I have my self-respect—something I realize I never had until now.

I hear Tori's voice before I see her, and my stomach backflips. I turn to find her walking my way with Brett and his family. I plaster on a smile. "Please," I say, motioning them to the backdrop.

Tori stands back. "You guys go on."

"Come on. I want you in the picture," Brett's mom says.

"I'm going to sit this one out."

The man I don't recognize says, "Why don't you do one with just you and your boys."

Brett's mom shrugs, and she, Brett, and his brother go and stand at the backdrop. She's in the middle, wrapping her arms around each of her sons, grinning like a proud mama bear.

Brett's brother won't look at the camera, but I get the feeling that's not anything unusual. Brett focuses on me with his expression impassive. His mom squeezes them both to her. "Y'all can at least pretend you love me." Both men soften, and Brett gives the smallest of smiles, but one that reveals his love for his mother.

My hand is so shaky I can barely take the picture. I snap several, hoping I get one that's not blurred. "That's it," I say, almost dropping the camera. "Um, please list your phone number or your email address in the tablet, then I will send these to you." Brett takes the tablet and taps into it.

"Thank you so much," Brett's mom says.

Tori stands by her, watching Brett like she's waiting for him. He sets the tablet down and then walks over. "Mom, I'd like you to meet Kylie."

His mom's face brightens. "Oh. Kylie. I'm so glad to meet you. I'm Melody."

Brett and Tori exchange a glance, and Tori looks like she's *sorry, not sorry*. It makes me wonder which one of them told his mother about me.

"Are you the resort's photographer?" she asks.

I give a nervous giggle. "Just for today. I work in Outreach."

"Oh, very good," she says, and by the look on her face, I may have scored a few points.

"You work at the hospital, right?" I say. "You're a patient care technician?"

She smiles. "I am."

"That sounds like rewarding work," I say.

"It can be. It can be exhausting work, too," she says, rolling her eyes but keeping her smile. She turns to the man. "This is Scott."

I shake the man's hand. "It's nice to meet you, sir."

Another family walks up to have their photo taken.

"We'll let you get back to work," she says. "I hope I'll see you again though?" She glances between Brett and me.

It's almost more than my heart can take. I just nod and say, "So nice to meet you." I retreat to my duties.

~

I CAN FEEL the toll the day has taken on me as we break down all the games and stations. My phone rings, and I shake my head because it's my dad. Of course he would call me on Family Day. I think the universe just wants to drive home the fact that I don't have one.

I answer. "Hi, Dad."

"How's my favorite daughter?"

I roll my eyes. "I'm fine."

"I hear you're better than fine."

I stop in my tracks, thinking about Joshua. We ended on a good note, but who knows what he went home and told my dad.

"I hear you've advanced to outreach director."

"Coordinator," I say.

"You'll be a director soon enough."

I'm so shocked from his positivity that I have to re-orient myself.

"I see that you're having Family Day down there today," he says.

"Oh, yeah?" I ask, a little confused.

"I'm on the resort's website."

I nod, even though he can't see me. "They do it once a year down here."

"While I understand why you didn't invite me, for the record, if you would have, I would've come."

I step farther away from the busy people cleaning up the area. I don't say anything, wondering if there's a trick coming.

"Kylie, honey, I'll admit that I'm not the most gracious loser. I'm used to getting what I want. You've always been so agreeable. When I saw you turning into a strong young lady, it threatened me. It's not easy for me to admit that, and it's taken some soul-searching, but I just want to tell you that I'm happy for you."

It feels like an ostrich has just launched itself off of my shoulders. "You mean that?"

"I do mean it. I was so scared of losing you, that in the process, I did just that."

I let out a sigh, not ready to give in yet, but I can feel myself caving.

"I know I'm a day late and many dollars short, but I'd like to help. What do you need?"

I smile to myself. "It turns out I don't need anything."

"That's my girl," he says.

I walk a few steps, letting silence sit between us, and then I say, "Maybe you can come visit another time?"

"I'd like that. Tell me about the job."

I glance at Bailey and Janelle, who look like they're wrapping things up. "I'm tied up right now, but can I call you later?"

"Sure, honey. I love you."

I press my hand against my heart, feeling myself decompress for the first time in months. "I love you, too, Dad."

I walk over to where Bailey and Janelle are and survey the empty pavilion area with them. "Ladies, I think this was a huge success," Janelle says.

"We had more people here than last year, didn't we?" Bailey asks.

"It definitely felt that way." Janelle turns to me. "You were such a great help. You better watch out. We're going to recruit you for PR."

"I'm just happy to be here," I say.

Janelle shoulders her purse. "That's it for me. I'll see you ladies on Monday."

"See you," we say, and I grab my bag from the pavilion stairs.

"So a few of us are going to Robert's boat this evening," Bailey says. "We'd like you to join us." She gives me a significant look.

My stomach flutters as the memory of the last time I was on that boat comes crashing in. "Um, is..." I don't know how to ask whether or not Brett's going to be there.

She takes my hand and squeezes it. "We *all* want you to be there." She nods at my bag. "Check your tablet."

She smiles and walks away, leaving me curious and even more anxious than I was when I started the day.

I fish the tablet out of my bag and scroll down to where Brett's family name is.

I'm an idiot. Can we talk?

I press the tablet to my chest, getting my second wind for the day.

As I walk up the dock, my heart gallops in my chest like it's striding to win the Kentucky Derby. I don't know what I'm walking into or who all is here, but it feels like change is on the horizon.

I cover my heart as Robert's boat comes into my sightline. It's draped with white lights and pink and white lilies. As I approach it, Bailey is ushering Cohen out the door. Her eyes go wide as she sees me. "We're just going to get some ice."

"Okay," I say, but I'm pretty sure I remember seeing an ice machine last time I was here.

I open the door to find Brett sitting on the couch with

his knee bouncing up and down as his mouth moves like he's talking to himself. He looks up at me and stands. "Hey."

"Hey," I say, glancing around, noting he's alone.

"Can we talk a minute?" he asks.

"Okay," I say. He indicates the couch, and I sit, clasping my hands together, mostly to stop them from shaking.

He faces me, looking like he's ready to run a marathon. "It doesn't take a rocket scientist to figure out that I've behaved poorly these past couple of months. I've been so angry with myself that I lost sight of how my own anger and isolation affect others. I don't know if you feel this way at all or not, but I want you to know that no part of me has blamed you for what happened that night. And I know that may sound assumptive to say. You may not have felt that way at all. But it's been brought to my attention that my selfish behavior affects others in ways that I don't realize." He looks me in the eye. "Do you mind if I ask how that night has affected you or if it has at all? And it's okay if it hasn't. I just—"

"Brett, it definitely has affected me. Of course it has. I've felt like my selfish behavior is why your grandmother is not with you anymore."

"It wasn't your behavior."

I hold up a hand up, indicating for him to let me finish, and he does.

"I didn't understand. You told me about your family and your grandma and about Matthew. But I interfered with that dynamic because I was selfish. I got caught up at work and didn't give you enough time during the week, and then when I saw you, I had all these raging hormones that felt like they took my whole body prisoner."

He looks down, his cheeks going red.

"I have a ton of guilt," I say. "I know you do, too. And I

know the burden you carry has got to be huge. I just want to make you feel better."

He shakes his head, looking away from me, reminding me of his brother. "I don't deserve you. I don't even deserve your friendship."

I take his hand. "You have my friendship. And you have much more if you'll take it from me."

He meets my gaze. "I haven't lost you?"

I shake my head, the pressure at the backs of my eyes releasing like a dam.

He cups the back of my neck and pulls me to him. His lips on mine send my body into orbit. He pulls away and then brings me to his chest, embracing me, warming my heart, and making me feel like I'm finally home.

He pulls away and takes my hands. "It's going to be a while before I'm healed from this, and a part of me will never heal."

"I understand that. But I want us to work on it together."

He nods. "Me, too. I love you, Kylie. I love you so much."

Tears come like a waterfall. "I love you, too," I say, barely getting the words out intelligibly.

He holds me again for a long moment, and then says, "I have something for us."

He stands, offering me a hand. I take it and follow him to the boat deck where we climb to the roof. A table and chairs are set up along with plates and drinks. "You did all this?" I ask.

"It was a group effort. Logan got the dinner from Big Fish, Cohen got the flowers from the horticulture stash, and Bailey bossed everyone around."

I laugh, my heart so full it's about to burst. "You have amazing friends."

"We have amazing friends." He points over my shoulder,

and I turn to find the whole group of them—Bailey, Logan, Cohen, Tori, Isaac, Simone, and Val watching us from a distance on the dock.

I cover my mouth and then my heart, trying to contain my love for all these people. I wave to them, and they wave back as they walk away. I turn to Brett. "We do."

We embrace again and hold on to one another with the seagulls and the ocean waves and my new family in my heart.

EPILOGUE
BRETT

Being back on the beach on a Saturday afternoon with all my resort friends is a step toward normalcy. I know I'll never feel a hundred percent back to normal, but trying to do stuff that makes me happy is starting to feel more right than wrong.

The guys and me finish up our game of volleyball and then head over to where the girls are lined up on the edge of the blanket with their toes in the sand. Kylie is telling a story about her next-door neighbor, who used to be a roadie for boy bands.

"When are you going to invite us over to your new place?" Isaac asks.

"It's tiny. I don't even know if we'd all fit in the living room together. We'd be on top of each other."

Logan waggles his eyebrows. "Sounds like a plan to me."

Kylie scrunches up her face. "Do you guys really want to see it?"

Everyone gives her their version of an enthusiastic yes. Kylie beams with pride. I love that she's got her own place, not just because it pulls her away from Jack Massey, but because of the woman she is becoming now that she's proven to herself that she doesn't need her father or anyone else to make it on her own.

"Tomorrow night then?" she asks, glancing around the group.

"Sunday night dinner," Cohen says. "I'm down."

"Family dinner," Bailey says, pulling Kylie in for a side hug.

Kylie looks so happy she might cry. When I think about how I almost lost her, I feel like I can't breathe for a second. But she's mine now, and I will never let her go again.

A group of people walking down the beach grabs my attention, and I see that it's Jack Massey and some of the other corporate drones. They take a spot near us, and then Easton throws a football to Jack. They head toward the water where they toss it back and forth to one another.

I glance over at Tori. She's engaged with the other girls, seeming oblivious to Jack's presence, but Tori is a really good actor.

I look between Jack and Kylie, thinking about how jealous I was of him when she was staying with him. But it was all for nothing. In fact, he was there for her when she needed someone. He was there for her when I wasn't. I walk toward him.

When Easton spots me coming, he tosses the football to me. I catch it and toss it back to him as I walk up next to Jack. One of the other guys in their group yells out to Easton, and he throws the ball to that guy. Jack turns to me, giving me a look like he's sizing me up. "Are you here to kick my ass or play football?"

"I'm here to say thank you."

Jack looks taken aback. "What did I do?"

"You took care of Kylie."

"I didn't really do much. Just gave her somewhere to stay."

"You also gave her your friendship at a time when she needed it." I look down, the shame overwhelming me. "I just couldn't be around her. But it wasn't her fault."

"You went through some traumatic shit," he says. "It's understandable."

"Well, thanks for not being a dick and trying to hook up with her."

"No problem," he says, swatting a bug off his arm.

I consider him. "Why didn't you make a move? Kylie looks like girls I've seen you with—tall, leggy, beautiful."

"It just wasn't like that with her. I don't know what else to say."

Jack's gaze goes to the line of girls, and more specifically, to Tori. She glances at us at that exact moment and then looks away like she's been caught.

This is where I should tell Jack that Tori's never gotten over him and that he should quit being an idiot and go talk to her, but Jack's a grown ass man. He can figure that shit out for himself.

"All right," I say and hold out my hand to him. He shakes it, looking me in the eye. I walk over to our group.

Kylie gets up and comes toward me, meeting me at the shore. "Did you play nice?"

"Believe it or not, I did."

She smiles. "The way the two of you shook hands, I thought maybe you decided to be BFF's again."

"One step at a time."

She kisses me. "I adore you, Brett Hargrove."

I slide my hand over her hip, running my thumb along the string on her bikini. "I'm pretty damn in love with you, too."

We kiss again, her lips on mine warming my whole body.

"Smile for the camera." We turn to see Bailey with her phone in the air, poised to take a picture. I pull Kylie close and she tilts her head against mine. Bailey grins at her phone. "You two are so crazy adorable."

"Let me see the picture," Logan says, grabbing for Bailey's phone. She snatches it away from him, and then he chases her up the beach.

Kylie turns back to me. "I really am the luckiest girl."

"You're not lucky. You're just someone who knows how to work her way into other people's hearts."

"I'm just glad to be in yours," she says, tapping my chest.

I grab her finger and kiss the tip. "Always."

Find out if Jack can win Tori back!

Up for Seconds is available now!

He won't get in her head again...

Tori Jacobs has spent the past year moving on from her intense relationship with Jack Massey, but now he's trying to win her back. His jealousy ruined them. They're too different, anyway. He's a stuffy, number-cruncher from a wealthy family, and she's a hot mess from a place that would make his family clutch their pearls. But Jack has never failed at anything in his life except for his relationship with her, and he doesn't intend to lose at that again.

Also Available from Melissa Chambers:

Destiny Dunes Series:
Down for Her: A Riches-to-Rags Steamy Romance
Up for Seconds: A Second Chance Steamy Romance
Coming Around: A Friends-to-Lovers Steamy Romance
In His Heart: A Harbored Secrets Steamy Romance
Over the Moon: A Forced Proximity Steamy Romance
Under the Stars: An Enemies to Lovers Steamy Romance

Broussard Brothers Series:
Grumpy Beignet Boss: A Second Chance Steamy Romance
French Quarter Flirt: A Friends to Lovers Steamy Romance
Bourbon Street Bachelor: An Enemies to Lovers Steamy
Romance
Frenchmen Street First: A First Love Steamy Romance

Love Along Hwy 30A Series:
Seaside Sweets: A Steamy Small Town Beach Read
Seacrest Sunsets: A Steamy Opposites-Attract Beach Read
Seagrove Secrets-A Steamy Brother's Best Friend
Beach Read
WaterColor Wishes: A Steamy Enemies-to-Lovers Romance
Grayton Beach Dreams: A Steamy May-December Romance
Rosemary Beach Kisses: A Steamy Single Dad Romance
Christmas in Santa Rosa: A Steamy Second Chance
Romance

Young Adult titles:
The Summer Before Forever (Before Forever #1)
Falling for Forever (Before Forever #2)

Courting Carlyn (Standalone)
Two Boy Summer (Standalone)

ABOUT THE AUTHOR

Melissa Chambers writes contemporary novels for young, new, and actual adults. A Nashville native, she spends her days working in the music industry and her nights getting lost in her characters. While she's slightly obsessed with alt rock, she leaves the guitar playing to her husband and kid. She never misses a chance to play a tennis match, listen to an audiobook, or eat a bowl of ice cream. (Rocky road, please!) She's a member of several online and local writers groups, all of which she treasures and is unendingly grateful for, and has served as president for the Music City Romance Writers.

BB bookbub.com/profile/melissa-chambers

a amazon.com/Melissa-Chambers/e/B00MRU380K

f facebook.com/MelissaChambersAuthor

instagram.com/melissachambersauthor